Starting with non-fiction, **Dianne Drake** penned hundreds of articles and seven books under the name JJ Despain. In 2001 she began her romance-writing career with *The Doctor Dilemma*. In 2005 Dianne's first Medical Romance, *Nurse in Recovery*, was published, and with more than 20 novels to her credit she has enjoyed writing ever since.

REUNITED WITH HER ARMY DOC

DIANNE DRAKE

MILLS & BOON

First published in Great Britain 2017
by Mills & Boon, an imprint of HarperCollins*Publishers*
1 London Bridge Street, London, SE1 9GF

Large Print edition 2018

© 2017 Dianne Despain

ISBN: 978-0-263-07287-7

MIX
Paper from
responsible sources
FSC
www.fsc.org
FSC™ C007454

This book is produced from independently certified FSC™ paper to ensure responsible forest management. For more information visit www.harpercollins.co.uk/green.

Printed and bound in Great Britain
by CPI Group (UK) Ltd, Croydon, CR0 4YY

To Nana & PopPop—
together through the eternities.

CHAPTER ONE

THE RADIO SCRATCHED out a sour little tune, one that sounded like it was on vinyl. Caleb's hand went automatically to the scan button because he wanted to hear something else. When Matthew was with him, it was always classical—a symphony or concerto from the only world his son knew. But when Caleb was alone, like today, he dialed straight into country. He loved the soulfulness of it. The expression. The heartaches, trials and tribulations. Things he could relate to in his own life.

Marrell, Montana, the sign ahead of him said, welcoming him back to the one place he'd thought he'd never live again. Visit, yes. More than a day or two…no. Not him. Not anymore. Too many childhood memories, too many difficult times. But never say never, right? Because here he was, right back where he'd started. Only this time with his son. Just the two of them. And, he was driving a beat-up old pickup truck that had come with the property he was renting. Plenty of dents, a fair share of rust, bumpy ride, but dependable. The same could be said of him. Plenty of dents—war wounds, physical and mental, plus a fair share of rust because, face it, at thirty-six, he wasn't getting any younger. And the bumpy ride—that was his life now.

So much had changed. It amazed him even thinking about it. Six years ago, he had been an army field surgeon, seeing active duty in off-and-on stretches, spending most of his time acting as the intermediary medical consultant and surgeon between combat injuries and the soldier's transport back home. Until two years into his duty when he, himself, had been the one on that transport, finding the end of his military medical career in a hospital rehab section, trying to relearn the use of an arm now held together with hardware.

Sighing, Caleb glanced at the time on his cell phone, and pressed the gas pedal a little harder. Marrell was about as big as a blink and here he was, on his first day at Sinclair Hospital, tooling through town so slowly he was in jeopardy of being late. First day on a new job in a new life, and he was unsure of himself. Unsure of his decision to move home, to start over here. But Hans Schilling tutored privately nearby, and the Schilling name was nothing to be sneezed at in the world of classical piano. Matthew needed that tutoring, so his list of "nevers" went by the wayside.

Also, being back home did come with some advantages. His family, the beautiful area... Yes, those were his own personal fond memories, and he was glad he did have some, because he had other memories, too. The dark, painful ones, where he'd been the odd kid out. And now Matthew could easily become the same.

Stopping his truck in front of the hospital, in a parking spot that was already labeled with his name, Caleb glanced at the sign over the front door, then glanced away. Was he really doing this? Really going to work at Sinclair Hospital? It used to be just a clinic—a lodge-type building sporting one doctor, two exam rooms, a makeshift lab and a tiny space for minor procedures. It had also been his safe haven as a kid. But Henry had added on a piece at a time to his clinic until he'd finally built a respectable regional hospital. Henry Sinclair—the doctor who'd delivered him, who'd introduced him to the world of medicine. Something that had turned into his passion at a very young age.

"You coming in?" Henry asked, knocking on Caleb's window. He was an affable-looking man. Large, broad smile, thick gray hair, keen gray eyes, rugged build. Except for his hair color, Henry hadn't changed in the thirty-six years he'd known him. Not true for Caleb, though. He was gaunt, could see it when he looked in the mirror. And he looked tired. Plus, there was no joy in his eyes like he saw in Henry's. Only a haunting reminder—

"Just indulging in a few memories of the place," Caleb said, stepping out of the truck. But the memories here were mixed. Good and bad. The good had helped build him into who he was today, the bad had worked against him for a long, hard time.

"It's changed a lot since you last worked here. Got forty-five beds now, an operating room for minor surgeries, and specialists coming in part-time. So, you could say we're almost well-rounded."

"Marrell's changed, too. It has more than two buildings. And did I notice a turnoff sign out on the highway." For a town where no one ever turned off.

Caleb locked the truck door behind him, wondering if people here still left all their doors unlocked, or had time finally caught up to this tiny little nowhere town? Nah, time hadn't caught up, he decided. Their doors were still unlocked.

"Population has almost quadrupled since you left. People are finding this a nice place to retire, or build a weekend cabin. Got a couple of movie stars with ranches nearby and, of course, Hans Schilling. Also, lots of beautiful wilderness still untouched, no one to bother you—"

"Meaning Marrell is finally on the map?" He fell into step with Henry, the way he'd often done when he'd been a kid, feeling so important in the middle of his insecure world.

He chuckled. "We've always been on the map, son. You just weren't looking at the right map."

In all fairness, that was true. He hadn't been, because he'd hated Marrell when he'd been young. It had been too confining, too limiting in what it had to offer. Especially for the genius kid who hadn't fit in. Then there was Leanne—

"So, tell me, Henry, how many patients can I expect to see daily?" He held the front door open and allowed Henry to enter the lobby in front of him. It was a well-appointed area, wide-open spaces, lots of wood structure. It resembled a mountain lodge more than a hospital.

"Maybe a dozen, on average. We've got people coming in from all over the area, and Dora Hanson over in Westslope is retiring shortly so, little by little, she's sending her practice to us."

"She's retiring?" He remembered her. She was a good doctor. Kind. Gave out huge lollipops to all the children. "Hard to imagine."

"When you get to that certain age…"

Dora Hanson, getting to that age. He still pictured her as forty, vibrant, cheery smile. Of course, she probably still pictured him as someone close to Matthew's age—five. Time did have a way of marching on when you weren't noticing. "I always liked her. She gave out better candy than you did."

Henry chuckled. "Of course, you would remember the important thing."

"To a young child, that lollipop *was* the important thing."

"Do you give out lollipops, Caleb?"

He didn't. His two years in a Las Vegas clinic had been so fast-paced, he'd barely had time to get the necessities done, let alone give out lollipops or even be the father Matthew needed. "Maybe I'll have to buy some," he said, suddenly feeling connected a little differently than he had only moments earlier. Back to his roots, back to some of the more traditional ways. Ways he hoped to give to his nontraditional son.

"Well, just so it won't come as a big shock to you when you hear it, Dora and I are getting married shortly."

That announcement snapped Caleb back to the present, and he blinked his surprise. "What?"

"Getting married and heading toward retirement while I'm still young enough to enjoy my new life with her." He pointed to a hall veering off the main waiting area, and both men headed in that direction. "Got some good fishing years left in me, and Dora and I want to travel, take in some sights we weren't able to see while we were in full-time practice."

"Who's going to run the hospital?" Caleb asked, even though he had a sinking feeling he already knew.

They stopped in front of a door that was marked "Family Practice Clinic," with the name "Dr. Caleb Carsten" already inscribed on a placard next to it. "I'm signing the place over to Leanne, but she's been telling me she doesn't want to move back here." He grinned. "Since she'll be the new owner, I suppose that will be her problem to figure out while I'm out on the river somewhere, casting my line."

Leanne Sinclair. The name from his past he wasn't sure he liked hearing again. Of course, working for her dad made it inevitable that he would, although he'd been trying not to think about it. *But working for her?*

Suddenly, Caleb was having second thoughts about being here. And third thoughts. For an instant, he wondered if he should simply get his old job back, and look for a different resolution in his life. Someplace where he didn't have to be around Leanne, or the memories she'd left him with, memories that once-upon-a-time had nearly destroyed him. Sure, they had been kids back then, but some hurts didn't go away. Instead, they lingered and festered like an open wound. *Leanne was his open wound.*

Leanne Sinclair leaned her head back against her chair and sighed. "All you have to do is say the word, and I won't go." She'd known that returning home might be a possibility, but now? She'd had four great months with Eric and, while she wasn't ready yet to call him the one, he was certainly settling in on that distinction. He'd asked her, two weeks into their relationship, to make it exclusive, and she'd agreed.

But now, her dad needed her home. Five hundred and eighty-two miles from Seattle, and from Eric. A nineteen-hour drive due to the rough terrain. Not so far in miles, but very far by the emotions when she really had none invested in Marrell, Montana. Hadn't for a long time.

And, while she was absolutely coming back to Seattle after she got the situation in Marrell sorted, she wasn't sure, yet, how everything was going to work. Her dad was going into semire- tirement with an eye toward full retirement in a year, and he was giving her his hospital. Not only that, but he wanted her to stay and run it.

Like that would ever happen.

"I'm waiting," she said to Eric, her eyes still closed.

"Going home's not such a bad thing, is it? And it's not like it's going to be forever."

That wasn't exactly what she'd wanted to hear from him. Somehow, in her mind, she'd expected him to ask her to stay. Or even beg her. Tell her he couldn't live without her, or didn't want to. But to suggest she should go?

"And it's not like Marrell's that far from Seat- tle," he continued. "We can meet up in the mid- dle somewhere, anytime we're both free."

She stared up at him. Eric Harrison was a

handsome man. Movie-star good looks. Black, wavy hair, green eyes, nice physique. "Are you saying you want me to go? Is that what I'm hearing?"

Eric, who was standing across from Leanne, leaned forward, placed the palms of his hands flat on her desk and shook his head. "Of course, I don't *want* you to go. But we don't all get the choices we like, do we?"

No, she hadn't expected this at all, and she was stunned by how quickly the hurt was bubbling up in her. "I don't understand. Since we're so new, I thought you'd want me to stay."

He chuckled. "Don't be so insecure. We'll make this work, no matter where you are."

"A long-distance relationship?"

"For three months. A lot of people do it for a whole lot longer than that. It's not so difficult these days."

"But I'm not a lot of people." And she wanted to stay close to her man. She also wanted him to want her to stay closer and, so far, Eric was avoiding that.

"No, you're not, or I wouldn't have been so attracted to you in the first place."

Maybe it was some undefined apprehension causing her to wonder if that attraction had been anything other than physical for him. Some stupid insecurity just now popping up. Because she was feeling apprehensive about going to Marrell. Not sure why, but her stomach was doing flip-flops, now that the plan was all but definite. "Can we try to schedule meeting somewhere two or three times a month?"

"Or more, if we can work it out." He reached over and squeezed her hand. "It's going to work, Leanne. You've got my promise."

Maybe she had his promise, but what she didn't have was his optimism. And she wasn't normally such a pessimist. But there was something about going home for three months...

"One year, ten months," Henry Sinclair stated emphatically. He and Leanne were strolling together through the halls of Sinclair Hospital, both wearing white jackets, both looking very doctorly.

"That long?" Leanne questioned. "I'd have sworn I came home sometime about a year ago." Her dad looked good. He claimed his health was great, and she trusted he wasn't lying to her. Plus, he was a man in love. After a lifetime of having no mother, at age thirty-six she was about to get one. Dora was nice. Leanne had known her all her life, and she was sure that her dad and Dora would be happy together. Maybe Dora would succeed in something where she'd failed— holding her dad's attention for more than a minute or two at a time. She hoped so.

"Nope. I marked it off on the calendar. One year and ten months, which you might as well call two years."

Admittedly, she hadn't been the most dutiful of daughters these past several years. First, because she just didn't like coming home. And second, because as her responsibilities and skills continued to move her forward in Seattle's medical mainstream, she was better able to forget Marrell. Some memories weren't as vivid, she was discovering now that she was back, and she was fine with that.

So, she was eager to get on with whatever she had to do so she could go back to her real life. To Eric. Because the farther she was away from him in miles, the further she felt distanced emotionally. The way she always had, in every other relationship, affair or friendship she'd attempted. Eric was her success. Her longest. Except Caleb, but that had been a kid thing, which didn't count. And now, she didn't want anything happening to what she had with Eric. But she was already beginning to feel the detachment, wondering if it had something to do with Marrell.

What was it about this place that made her feel so uncomfortable?

"So, about the hospital, Dad…"

"I know. You don't want it. Don't want to move back here."

"None of that's changed." Couldn't, wouldn't.

"You always knew it would be yours, Leanne. This shouldn't come to you as a surprise."

"It doesn't. But I'm not…" She drew in a deep breath. This was difficult because she didn't want to hurt him. While her feelings for her dad were strained, there was nothing malicious in her. Nothing that made her want to punish him. Living how she wanted would, though, as that didn't include her dad's dream. "Since I'm *not* moving back, my thought was to own it from a distance and trust the daily operations to someone else." She could tell by the disappointment registering on her dad's face it wasn't what he'd hoped for. But it was the best she could do. "I don't fit in here, Dad." Hadn't since she'd been a kid. In fact, the most solid memory of her childhood was her plan to get away from Marrell as soon as she could.

She and Caleb running away together… They were only nine or ten when they'd planned it, but it was a plan that had always stayed alive in her with, or without, Caleb. "I've lived away from Marrell almost as long as I lived here, and the blood in my veins runs pretty thin when it comes to my sentiment for this place."

Finally arriving at her dad's office, she followed him in, immediately went to the cushy leather chair across the desk from him and sat down. Same chair she'd always sat in. Same decorations. Fishing lures and poles hung on the wall, photos of fishing trips filled spaces where fishing gear did not, along with old photos of babies he'd delivered and patients he'd cured. *No pictures of her.* Bookshelves on the south wall were filled with medical volumes and books about—yes, fishing. All of him, none of her. Such a stark reminder of what she'd never had.

"There's nothing I can say or do to change your mind?" Henry asked, dropping down into the well-worn leather chair behind his desk.

"I took a three-month leave of absence instead of resigning my position in the hospital. That'll give me plenty of time to get to know Sinclair, and find the right person to take over."

"But you'll still own it?"

No, she didn't want that burden either. But the hospital was almost a family legacy, so it only seemed right that she should keep it in the family...for a while. "I'll still own it," she replied.

"Well, I do have a new hire who might be good to take over. Caleb Carsten. He's been here three weeks, just moved back to Marrell himself."

"Caleb's back?" she asked, totally shocked. Caleb—her first love when she'd been five. First heartbreak much later. "I'm surprised," she said tentatively, not sure how to react. To love him being here because he might be the solution to her problem, or hate it because he'd quit being her friend when she'd most needed one? Maybe she'd be indifferent since all that was a lifetime ago. "He hated it here. That was something we both had in common." And it almost felt personal that he'd changed his mind and come back.

"Well, hate or not, he's renting the old Wilson place out on Bentwood Road, and if his plans work out, he'll probably buy it."

Caleb settling down here? Hard to imagine. So, what was behind it? "He's a surgeon, isn't he? Why would a surgeon want to work here? We don't do major surgeries."

"Because he's in family practice now. Got wounded in Afghanistan, can't operate. He had to change direction."

Well, Caleb had always been about changing direction, hadn't he? Still, changing direction toward Marrell? Why here, specifically? "Why didn't you tell me he'd come home?" she asked, dragging up old memories of Caleb Carsten.

He'd been a little on the rough side, looks-wise. Sandy-blond hair, always a little bit long and unkempt, blue eyes... Sort of a solitary boy. Awkward. Odd. Often in trouble. Smart. Probably the smartest kid she'd known. So full of promises she'd bought into when she was so young she hadn't understood all the things that had kept him apart from the other kids in town.

"Because I wasn't sure he'd accept my offer to work here permanently, and I'm still not sure he'll stay. So, I decided to wait until he'd made up his mind about Marrell before I said anything."

"Meaning you kept me out of the loop, even though you want me to take over the very same loop you're keeping me out of?" Some things never changed. Her dad had *always* overlooked her. Even when she'd tried hard to get him to notice, he never had. In fact, there'd been times when she'd believed he'd favored Caleb over her.

"I thought if you knew Caleb was back, you might not come. You two didn't have a happily-ever-after ending, you know."

"He was a bad kid, Dad. Got into trouble. Got

put in jail." *Replaced me whenever you'd let him.* "What was I supposed to do? Give up on everything I wanted and hope he would have a miracle transformation? And you're right, if I'd known he was back, working here in family practice, I probably wouldn't have come. Not because I don't want to see him but because he's capable of doing everything you expect me to do and, probably, secretly want him to do more than you want me to."

"What's that supposed to mean?" Henry asked, looking over the top of his glasses at her.

"It means Marrell isn't big enough to support both Caleb and me, especially in the same field. Since he apparently wants to be here, and I don't..." She shrugged.

"But the hospital's yours, all except signing the papers, which are being drawn up right now."

"You know I don't want to run it, Dad, or work in it. I'll own it, but that's all, as I have a different life than that." He wasn't listening to her, though, like the way he'd never listened to anything she'd ever said. Still, she wasn't giving up on this. Especially now that Caleb had entered the mix and offered her the possibility of something she hadn't expected—a good, workable solution.

"Then it will have to be your decision to turn the day-to-day operations over to somebody else."

She wasn't going to engage. They'd had this discussion—*argument*—many times over the past year. He knew where she stood, and nothing about that had changed. But Caleb…now, that added a whole new dimension to this argument. Maybe he *could* be the one to take over. Hopefully, buy her out sometime in the future. It was certainly a plan worth considering. "Which I will certainly do. So, how was Caleb wounded?" she asked, not sure what to expect.

"Shot in the shoulder. Shattered the bone, caused some neurological damage. Not enough to cause a lot of disability but enough to keep him out of the OR."

That was too bad, because she imagined Caleb would be good at anything he did. She was sure he'd have been a great surgeon. "And he's back in Marrell, why?"

"To raise his son. To be closer to his family, so they can help him."

"Then he's a single father?" That was something she hadn't expected. Somehow, she didn't picture Caleb as the father type.

"To a five-year-old."

"No mother in the picture?"

"Not that I'm aware of. But Caleb's a very good dad. Dotes on his son."

"I don't suppose I would have expected that from someone like him." Because she still pictured him as the one who stood apart from everybody else. The one being cuffed and carted off to jail. Which was, in fact, the last time she'd ever seen him.

"Someone *like* him, Leanne? Caleb was always a nice boy. A little troubled, yes, but he had potential. Went into the army after he was released from detention, got himself through college and med school. Then turned his life into something successful."

"I guess that makes sense, seeing how he would come to the hospital and follow you around all the time. *And all the attention you gave him.*"

That he hadn't given her. "Anyway, I'll catch up with him as soon as I can. Maybe ask him about taking over admin duties at Sinclair."

"Let him settle in first. Figure out if he's going to stay or not."

"You mentioned that before, that he might not stay."

"If Matthew doesn't get into Hans Schilling's school, he might not."

"The orchestral conductor who runs that school for child prodigies? Matthew is a musical prodigy?"

"From what I've heard. And that's the real reason why Caleb came home. Sure, having his family here for Matthew was a big incentive, but Hans Schilling was the real draw."

"Well, I'm not going to promise I'll wait before I start pressing him, because I have a life to get back to. But first I'd like to talk to him—for old times' sake." Not that she really recalled many of those old times since she'd been more focused on how she was going to make new times for herself.

"He's in this morning." Henry glanced at his

watch, saw that morning had slipped into noon. "Actually, you'll probably find him in the cafeteria right about now. Eating lunch."

"Then I'm on my way to the cafeteria. Care to join me?"

Henry shook his head. "I'm taking off early today. Meeting up with Dora, and we're going fishing. Do you want to join us for dinner tonight?"

"Fresh catch?" she asked, standing up.

"Whatever we can come up with. Dora makes this great frying batter..." He licked his lips. "You know she's going to make me fat, don't you?"

Leanne walked around the desk, bent down and gave her dad a kiss on his forehead. Even though they had their differences, some of them severe, she loved the old man. Admired him for his dedication to his work. He was a great doctor all the time, and a not-so-great father some of the time. In the scheme of things, she supposed he did the best that he could. "You haven't gained a pound in all the years I've known you and I don't think Dora's going to change that," she said. Then she went off in search of Caleb.

Caleb's first inclination was to look away when he noticed Leanne coming toward him. But that was the sixteen-year-old boy in him reacting. Apparently, when it came to Leanne, he was much closer to being that sixteen-year-old boy than he was a thirty-six-year-old man, because he did glance away about the same time his heart did a little clutch. So, he fixed his attention on the clock above the cafeteria cash register. Got involved in some heavy-duty studying of the way the hand that counted the seconds jerked as it ticked from moment to moment.

"Caleb?" she said, stopping directly in front of him, extending her hand to him. "How are you?"

He glanced up at her, smiled politely, stood, and accepted her handshake. "Leanne," he responded, then allowed himself a two-second appraisal of her, from head to toe. *Beautiful* was the word that first popped into his mind. Then *stunning*. Followed by *caution*. All while the jerky hand of the clock ticked loud enough to taunt him and cause him to sweat.

She let go of his hand and returned the same stare he'd just given her. Only, a little longer than two seconds. "I had no idea you'd come back to Marrell. Odd coincidence we're both here at the same time, isn't it?" she finally said.

She looked like she wanted to sit down with him. Had her hands on the back of the chair, ready to pull it out from the table. Problem was, he wasn't ready to have her there. Wasn't ready to have her attempt polite conversation or reminiscences. Wasn't ready for *anything*, where Leanne Sinclair was concerned. "I suppose it was bound to happen at some point, since you're going to be my new boss." Said deliberately and stiffly because he didn't want to leave the impression that he wanted to be friendly. Not with her.

Despite his best efforts to put up an almost visible wall between them, she pulled out the chair and seated herself across from him. Looking too damned pleasant. "Yeah, well, Dad and I have a difference of opinion on that. Which I don't want to talk about right now. Instead, tell me all about yourself."

He sat back down, looked down at the half-eaten Cobb salad sitting in front of him, then pushed it away. Suddenly his appetite was gone. "Not much to tell." At least, not much to tell *her*.

She adjusted in her chair, folded her hands on the table in front of her and stared him straight in the eyes. "Dad says you have a little boy?"

"Matthew. He's five. Closer to six now."

"It's hard to believe that you—that *we've* gotten that old. Last time I talked to you, you were what? Sixteen? Seventeen? And now you're a dad?"

"Yep. I'm a dad," he said, his voice still purposely stiff.

"Are you OK, Caleb?" she asked. "You seem… quiet."

"Just thinking about all I've got lined up for the afternoon." Not true, but it sufficed as the truth because what point was there in being blunt? Or telling her that he didn't want to be anywhere near her? Their close proximity was inevitable, at least for now, so why make it more difficult than it already was?

"Need some help? I don't have anything to do, and I'd be glad to pitch in."

"No. I'm fine. Only have a half-dozen patients scheduled, and I don't have anyone admitted to the hospital right now, so I'm good. But...thanks." She was trying so hard to break through to him, it almost made him feel bad that he was keeping his distance. But he didn't trust Leanne. He'd learned his lesson with her years ago, and it had been a hard one to learn—that life, and people, could be cruel. She'd shown him that, and he had no reason to believe she'd changed. Of course, there was no reason to believe she *hadn't* changed either. Consequently, he was fresh out of benefits-of-the-doubt where Leanne, or women in general, were concerned. She'd hurt him once too many times to yield even an inch for her. So had his ex-wife.

While the hurt was still fresh with Nancy, and Matthew was a constant reminder of that, going on to twenty years was a long time to hold on to all that hurt from Leanne. So, maybe it was just the whole relationship thing in general that he didn't want anywhere near him. At least, that was the thought he held on to when he did the polite thing and went to get her a glass of iced tea. Extra lemon, one artificial sweetener—something he shouldn't remember from the old days, yet did. But why? Caleb blew out a heavily frustrated breath as he carried her tea back to their table; impatient with himself for hanging on to such a trite little detail among a barrage of so many other larger, more impactful ones.

"Thanks for the tea," she said after taking her first sip. "I'm surprised you remembered how I take it."

"It came back to me," he lied. There were many things about Leanne he'd never forgotten. The way she tilted her head slightly to the right when she laughed. Or entered a room with such purpose she drew everybody's attention without even trying. Even the virulent expression that came over her when she was getting ready to put him down in front of his friends. Make fun of him. Lead him on, only to humiliate him.

"I know we weren't great friends back when

we were teenagers," she said, "but it's nice seeing you again. I've lost touch with pretty much everybody else. So, what have you been doing with yourself all these years...besides being a doctor and a dad? I heard you were in the military?"

Well, he did have to hand it to her. She was trying hard to be friendly. But it was difficult buying into something he didn't trust. Difficult buying into that friendliness. "Went into the Army after jail. They put me through med school, then I went to a base hospital in Germany, as a surgeon. By the time I was thirty-one, I'd met Nancy, was well on my way to being a dad, and before my first anniversary in Germany, I was newly married and newly deployed to Afghanistan.

"My first deployment was short because they let me go back to Germany for Matthew's birth. Then sent me back into combat when he was three months old. I was pretty successful in battlefield surgery there for nine months, then got wounded, then sent back to Germany to rehab and got divorced since she'd decided she didn't like being tied down. When the military sent me stateside, I rehabbed a little more in Boston and concluded I'd never be a surgeon again, not that I'd had much time to be one before. So, off to California to rehab for a few more months, then took a job there, hated it. Went to Houston, hated it. Philadelphia...the same.

"Finally, by the time Matthew was three and I was beginning to realize he needed stability, I landed a good job in Vegas, and settled down. But it was a horrible life for Matthew, who was getting old enough that his surroundings were making a difference. He didn't get to go out and play. His musical talent was beginning to appear but there was no one to guide it. No friends. Plus, his intellect set him apart from just about everything and everyone, and he was becoming a very unhappy, sullen little guy.

"So... Marrell. Primarily because Hans Schilling was here, and I want Matthew in his program."

"Then you didn't come back only because you wanted to come home?"

"I've been reading about Schilling for two

years. Wasn't thrilled that he'd ended up in Marrell, since I didn't want to end up here. But it is what it is. You have a kid, you turn your life inside out for him." It all sounded so cut-and-dried, even though it was anything but. And it tumbled out in far more abundance than he would have liked, and much too easily to be comfortable with.

"Sounds like quite a…journey. For both of you."

It was. A very rocky one because he was scared every step of it. Scared for Matthew, who needed more stability than he thought he could give. Scared for himself because every moment of every day he wondered if he was good enough to parent Matthew. "It is, but I'm hoping Marrell's our last stop. So, how about you? What have you been doing with yourself all these years?" He asked, not because he cared so much, but because he wanted to focus his thoughts elsewhere. Get rid of the ones that plagued him day in, day out.

"Pretty much med school, then medical practice. A couple of promotions. One I backed out of because it didn't suit me. Haven't had time for anything else."

"Then you're not married?" He wasn't sure why he'd asked because he didn't care.

She laughed. "Not yet, but..." She smiled, shrugged, then took a sip of tea. "I always knew you were going to be a doctor. Knew I was, too. But both of us here, back in Marrell..."

"I'm here because most everything I do now is for Matthew. No other reason." He wanted to be clear about that. Wanted her to know he made time for little else. Because, if she was looking for a friendship, or anything else from him...

"It was difficult on Dad, raising me alone, so I'm sure it's just as difficult for you. I'd like to meet him sometime, if we can arrange it."

She sounded sincere, and the gentleness in her eyes wasn't the same look he'd gotten used to seeing there all those years ago. "He's not settling in too well yet. My parents have him while I'm at work, and I have him the rest of the time, and he's just not finding his niche here."

"But if he gets on with Hans Schilling, I'm sure that will help him find his place. It's got to be difficult for him, all these changes he's gone through at such a young age. When I was his age, I don't think I'd ever been any farther away than Saka'am, or Westslope."

"He's been cool with the travel part. He's a lot like I was, though. Too smart to fit in. Always trying to wrap himself in his own little world."

"When you were a kid, I remember you used to like to hang out at the hospital and read Dad's medical texts for fun. You'd sit in his study for hours, reading, all wrapped up in a cocoon you'd built around yourself to shut people out."

"Matthew does that with his practicing."

"What does he do for fun?" she asked.

"He considers what he's doing fun. Like I said, Matthew is…serious. Too smart for his own good, too talented for his age, and the things that are fun for him are all tied up in that. Probably too much, which is why I'm hoping Schilling will accept him, because I think training tailored specifically for Matthew's talents will help him see there's more to life than his studies and his music."

"He needs to have the kind of fun we did back

then," she said, sounding as if she was trying to convince herself. "Remember how I always looked forward to seeing you?"

Seriously, that's what she remembered? That, and not the rest of it? How convenient, not dwelling on the way she'd treated him. But why? Because she wanted something from him again? The way she always had in the past? Ask for something, lead him on with expectations, then smash him to bits? "Yeah, good times," he said, trying not to sound too bitter even though, to his own ears, his words came out, as they said, as bitter as gall. "That was a long time ago, Leanne. I try not to dredge up old memories."

"Me neither, to be honest. All I wanted was to get out of Marrell. I think everything I did from the age of thirteen or fourteen was centered on that."

Or humiliating him. "But you're back. So, are you going to stay?"

"No. But Dad's trying hard to convince me to."

"He *is* pretty set on having you run the hospital."

"I know. But *I'm* set on getting someone else

to do it for me so I can go back to Seattle. Which isn't what Dad planned for me, and it's really causing me a lot of conflict because I don't want to hurt him. But I don't want to get hurt in this either."

"You coming home is all he's talked about ever since I got here," he said, taking a sip of his coffee.

"Well, times are changing and that's going to include my dad, who's totally resisted change pretty much as long as I've been alive. I'm worried about him, though."

Yes, times did change but, fundamentally, did people? *This* Leanne seemed nicer than the one he remembered. She seemed more genuine. Closer to the younger one, the little girl who'd been his friend for a time. Or was it all a deception, the way Nancy had been a deception? Thinking about all those pretexts in his life and how they'd hurt him, Caleb forced himself to smile. "Well, times may change everywhere else, but I wonder if they ever do in Marrell."

Leanne laughed. "Not so much. Mrs. Purcell still runs the grocery, Mr. Merrick is still the only mechanic in town, the post office is still in the back room of the hardware store. But there's a health club now, and the hospital. I suppose everything gives way to progress at some point, don't you think?"

Despite his feelings, Caleb chuckled. "And there's a stoplight on Main Street, and a coffee shop and even a movie theater."

"Second-run movies, though," she said, wrinkling her nose as she smiled.

"So, Seattle?" he asked, to get his mind off the past and the comfort beginning to set in that he simply didn't want there. "Never been."

"It's a nice place. Home. Career."

"Good life?"

She frowned, and paused a moment. "Most of the time, yes. I have a pretty good life."

"Which you don't want to change by moving back to Marrell."

"Something like that. And *that* brings me to the point of this conversation. Since you're staying, or thinking about staying, would you consider running the hospital?"

So that's what it was, Caleb thought. Step one. She wanted something.

"Maybe even look at buying it sometime in the future?"

Step two: lead him on with an expectation. "Buying it?"

"Something I don't want Dad knowing just yet. I have some plans…nothing solid, but I may be making a big change in my life, and it's all about being in Seattle. Not here."

"Would congratulations be in order?" he asked, waiting for step three to drop down on him. Because it would. It always had with her.

She shook her head. "Not yet. Eric's been offered a big promotion, and we want to make sure he's settled into that before we take the next step. So, the timing for that is a little off right now. But in a while…"

Caleb shook his head, and blew out a long breath. Well, her steps were out there. At least, most of them. And he hadn't had to wait too long. But he had some steps of his own to take and, until Matthew was settled, he wasn't sure in which direction they were going. "Let me think about it." Because if it was a legitimate offer, it was interesting. Even tempting. But he wasn't going to allow himself to buy too far into it, as he'd bought too far into her so many times before. Still, she did need someone here. So maybe... "I'm not making any permanent decision until I find out what's going to happen with Matthew. If Schilling accepts him, we stay. If he doesn't, we'll probably move on until we find the place he needs."

"I understand, and I won't press you for an answer, because I know what I'm proposing is a pretty major life-changer. So, take all the time you need. In the meantime, Dad's going to have a fish fry tonight. Care to come? Maybe we can reminisce about old times."

"I usually have plans with Matthew every evening." That was the truth. The other truth was, he still didn't want to reminisce about anything with Leanne, even if they'd just shared a few nice moments. What was there to reminisce about, besides memories of hurtful events?

"Then breakfast some morning? We could

meet at Millie's Diner down on Main Street, and have some of her world-famous pancakes."

"Don't eat pancakes. And it takes me a while to get Matthew ready in the morning so he can spend the day with his grandmother."

The smile on Leanne's face finally melted, replaced by a look of confusion. "You don't want to get together with me, do you? Did I do something to offend you?"

Too many things to discuss. Too many memories he didn't want to deal with. Nancy had wiped him out and he didn't want to step back into the ring to take a beating from another contender. "Look, Leanne. I'm busy right now. I'm trying to settle into a new life, set up a home, adjust to a new job, get Matthew situated… I've got a lot going on, and not enough time to get everything done." That much was true. He didn't. "So, since the only thing you could possibly want from me has to do with the job, drop into my office, ask Betty, the clinic's secretary, to find a spot in my schedule for you, then put your name in it."

"You used to be friendlier, Caleb," she commented, pushing back her tea, then standing.

"I also used to be more gullible. But like you said, times have changed, and I'm part of that change."

"What's that supposed to mean?" she asked him.

"Whatever you want it to mean." With that, he picked up his lunch tray, carried it over to the dirty dish area, set it down and left the cafeteria. Didn't look back. Wasn't even tempted to. But it did surprise him how all that water he'd thought had long since flowed under the bridge hadn't flowed as far as he'd thought it had.

CHAPTER TWO

WHAT SHE'D PLANNED and what she got were two entirely different things. Funny, she didn't remember Caleb being so cool. And he *was* cool—almost cold. She recalled him being a nice boy, one she'd had a crush on when she'd been little. His intellect, his humor... Then, when he'd got a little older, he'd turned wild. Gotten himself in a lot of trouble. But it seemed he'd worked through all that, because look at him now—to all appearances a great dad, and a great doctor, according to her dad. Well, time had a way of changing people. She certainly wasn't the same person she'd been whilst growing up in Marrell. That girl had been so unsettled. This one knew her place.

"He wasn't friendly at all, Dad," she commented to Henry, who was headed out the front door of his cabin on his way to meet Dora. Leanne was sitting in the porch swing, looking out over the meadowlands to the south, enjoying the nothingness of the moment. She didn't get too many of those in her life, and this one was nice. "Cordial, and having a hard time maintaining that."

Henry stopped at the edge of the porch, at the top of the wooden stairs leading to the path below, then turned to face her. "Don't know what to tell you, Leanne. He's been very pleasant to me, and to everybody else around here. But he's got some bad years behind him, so maybe that's what you're seeing coming out. Or maybe he was only having a bad afternoon."

"No. This went beyond a bad afternoon. There was something else going on, something I can't explain." And it made her wonder if she did want him to run her hospital after all. Of course, who knew what had gone on in his life? Maybe her dad was right. Maybe she was catching a glimpse of his past. Whatever the case, until she knew more, she would give him the benefit of the doubt and keep the offer open.

But what if she'd seen his real personality?

"Want me to have a talk with him?" Henry asked, appearing impatient to hop down those steps and be on his way. "See if I can figure out what's bothering him?"

She shook her head. "No. It's his business, and it's not my place to interfere. If he wants to talk, he can, but I won't force him into it." Because she didn't like being forced into something she didn't want to talk about, or admit, or do. A couple of months back she'd been promoted to the head of family practice, then discovered she hated being in charge. She wanted to go back to her old position where she dealt directly with her patients, knew their names and recognized faces, and didn't have to contend with budgets and scheduling, personnel conflicts and solutions. So, she'd stepped down, returned to what she loved best.

Eric didn't understand, though, because he craved leadership and authority. Consequently, they'd argued for days. He'd wanted her to keep the promotion. She hadn't. Simple as that then, simple as that now. She hated being pushed by him, hated pushing just as much, and she wasn't about to do that to Caleb. "Anyway, have a good time, Dad. Give Dora my love and tell her we'll get together soon. I think I'm going to pull some late hours working tonight, so maybe we can figure out something for later this week."

Henry scooted across the porch, gave Leanne a quick kiss on the cheek, then practically ran down the steps and out to his truck, like a man in love who was bursting to see his woman. It was kind of cute, she thought, a little envious that no one had ever been that eager to see her. Except Caleb, when they'd been kids. And that didn't count.

Leanne spent the next hour in her dad's home office, staring at a pile of folders, each one containing something she needed to read. Yes, her dad kept his records the old-fashioned way, even though the hospital had upgraded to a nice computer system, and she'd been urging him to do the same at home. "Just read them," she told herself, as she picked up a particularly fat one, stared at it for a moment, then tossed it back into the pile.

So, what was bugging her? Being home again?

Missing Eric? Caleb's aloof reaction to her? She didn't know, didn't particularly care because, true to her sentiments toward admin work, she wasn't in the mood to get down to business. Which meant all the paperwork confronting her got shoved aside for the time being, and she went to fix herself a cup of hot tea instead.

As the tea kettle whistled, Leanne glanced at her watch, saw that it was almost three o'clock, and decided it was time to refocus. Maybe text Eric. Right now, he would have finished up with his two-thirty appointment and be on his way to a half-hour break. Same routine every day. Never varied. In his office, lock the door, Do Not Disturb.

But this afternoon she wanted to disturb, so she pulled out her phone and texted.

Video chat coming up. Head to your computer.

She waited a moment for his response, but it didn't come, so she tried another text.

Eric, where are you?

This time she took a smiling selfie and attached it. But there was still no response. So...

Eric? You there?

Two minutes later came a reply.

Give me ten, babe. Tied up now.

She waited ten, wondering why he was tied up on what was supposed to be his break, then pulled out her personal laptop, since her dad's computer had been around since the dinosaurs, and connected to Eric. Her first reaction when his face came on screen—he looked frazzled. Flushed. Hair mussed, a little sweaty. Her second, he worked too hard. "I miss you," she started.

"Miss you more," he responded, looking past the computer camera to what would be the office door. "How's Marrell?"

"Small. Am I interrupting something?" she asked, noting how preoccupied he seemed.

"No. Just wrapping up some work. Ready to give you my undivided attention now. Anyway, you'll do fine there. Just start counting off the days until you come back to me." And finally, he gave her that smile, the one she'd always counted on to make her feel better.

"Easier said than done," she said, relaxing back into her chair. For whatever reason, she'd been a little edgy going into this chat, but seeing Eric's smile fixed all of that. "Especially when every day is going to be the same as the one before and the one after."

"Can't be that bad."

"It would be better if you were here." Even though he'd hate the place. Eric had no patience for small towns, small hospitals, small anything.

"It would be better if you were *here*," he countered. "So, tell me what's happened that's got you upset? And before you ask how I know, I can see it in your beautiful face. That little worry line between your eyes that pops up occasionally is popping, and it concerns me, Leanne. I don't like seeing you that way."

"I'm fine, Eric. Just a little stressed-out. But dealing with it." She reached up to feel for that worry line and, sure enough… "I met with an old friend today."

"Boyfriend?" Eric asked.

"No, nothing like that. We were friends when we were younger, that's all." Good friends for a while. "When I was five."

Eric chuckled. "Let me guess. He's seen what a beautiful woman you've grown into and he wants you back."

She shook her head. "Hardly. He's not very… friendly."

"So, what did your unfriendly *friend* do that's causing that wrinkle?"

"Actually, I don't know." And she didn't. It had been a strange meeting. "But I got the impression he wanted to get away from me as fast as he could."

"Why would any man in his right mind want to get away from you?"

"Just preoccupied, I think. He's heading up our family practice clinic here. He's also a war vet and a single father. I just…just expected him to be a little more open, or friendly."

"Well, we all have our stories, don't we?" He shifted in his chair, and glanced away from the monitor for a moment. Then back at her. "Our secrets, our excuses. So just allow the man his privacy, babe. I'm sure he needs it, for whatever reason."

Eric was right, of course. Whatever had caused Caleb to be the way he was, it was none of her business. In fact, the only thing that *was* her business was if he'd be suitable to head the hospital. "I asked him to take over here. Dad says he's qualified, and that would certainly be a great solution for me."

He grinned knowingly, arching sexy eyebrows. "It would get you back here to me quicker. I don't know how I'm going to go three months without you, even if we do get to meet in the middle from time to time, as we'd planned."

"Like next weekend?" Their first planned get-together. She'd made reservations at a quaint little bed-and-breakfast, and if things well…

"Afraid I've got to change that. I'm going to cover for one of the doctors here who needs the time off."

"But you need the time off, too," she protested.

"I do. But this comes with the job."

"Well, then, darn the job," she said, not even

trying to hide her disappointment. "What about the weekend after?"

"Not sure yet. I may have to represent the hospital at a conference, and if I can't get someone to go in my place, I'll be running down to Portland to do it myself. But maybe the second weekend of next month?"

"That's four weeks, Eric! I thought we were going to do better than that."

"Schedules happen, babe. You know that."

Yes, she did. And they always seemed to happen with Eric. *A lot.* "So, in the meantime…"

"Send me sexy selfies."

She forced a laugh. "What would the good people of Marrell think, if they knew?"

"That your man misses you in ways they've probably never even thought of."

It had been three days since Leanne had asked him to take charge of the hospital, and he'd been successful in avoiding any thought of it as the clinic had suddenly turned busy. Good excuse for putting it out of his mind, he decided while he escorted Mrs. Gentry down the hall to the reception area to schedule her next appointment. "Like I told you, it's not serious—yet. It's poison ivy, and the shot I've given you should start to clear it up, plus the pills I've prescribed will finish that. But you've got to take those pills," he warned the woman, fighting to hold his concentration. This past hour, Leanne had crept into his thoughts more than he was comfortable with. Her changes. His trust issues. Especially way she looked... And while his patient's condition was annoying to her, it just wasn't enough to hold his undivided attention. "Do you understand me? Your poison ivy is close to spreading to your eyes, and if that happens, it will turn into a serious situation."

"I'll do my best, Caleb," she told him, then reached up and patted him on the cheek. "You've grown up to be such a nice, polite boy. I always thought you had it in you to do good things. Even when you were acting out the way you did."

Sally Gentry was his grandmother's next-door neighbor. He'd played in her yard, eaten her homemade cookies, drunk her lemonade. Now he was her doctor, and she'd brought him cookies and lemonade today. "Just take care of yourself. Promise me?" It was tough treating old friends, knowing things about them that their doctor didn't have a right to know. He wondered how Henry had done that for the past forty years, how he'd separated the doctor from the friend or neighbor. Wondered if he could. Or if the town would let him, considering how most of them remembered him, remembered what he'd done.

"Ruth and I are cooking together tonight, if you'd like to come over for dinner." Ruth Carsten was his grandmother, and she and Sally spent a lot of time together now that they were both widows. "We're fixing your favorite fried chicken."

"I appreciate the offer, Mrs. Gentry, but Matthew and I have other plans." Actually, they didn't. But a night spent with two octogenarians fussing over him wouldn't sit well with Matthew, especially when all he wanted to do with his evenings right now was learn Chopin's Fantaisie-Impromptu, Opus 66, for his upcoming audition with Hans Schilling. Caleb didn't want to interrupt his son's regular habits any more than they'd been disrupted by moving here. "Send my love to my grandmother, though, and tell her Matthew and I will drop by in a couple of days."

Patients came and went for the next couple of hours, and Caleb kept himself busy, all the while trying not to think about the jerk he'd made of himself with Leanne. And make no mistake about it, he'd been a real jerk. Rude. Almost hostile. He'd known their meeting would be inevitable, and difficult, but he'd reckoned he'd put away some of his teenage feelings for her a long time ago. Had hoped that he wouldn't react to her the way he had the last time they'd seen each other—the day when he'd been hauled out of Marrell in handcuffs, in the back of a police car.

But no. One look at her, and he'd turned right back into that hurt teenager who'd let himself become the object of some serious bullying. And her plaything. Good old Caleb, there when she'd needed him, rejected when she hadn't. Made fun of in all those times in-between. Apparently, where Leanne was concerned, he hadn't moved too far away from the boy who'd been too hurt and confused to know how to respond. He wasn't sure he knew how, even now.

What surprised him most, though—totally shocked him—were the other feelings coming to surface. Ones where all he'd wanted was her attention. Ones that had carried him from a little-boy crush into a teenage heartbreak over a love he couldn't have. He'd hated her for what she'd done to him, but he couldn't help loving her at the same time. And some of those feelings were churning up in him now. Not that he loved her anymore, because he didn't. But the memories of that young love were surprisingly vivid, and stirring.

"I'm out of here," he told Betty, his secretary, on his way through the door, still trying to shake off all images of Leanne. He needed to concentrate on Matthew now. Not her. "Have a good evening."

"You, too, Caleb."

He smiled at her use of his name. Everyone in town knew him or his family, and everybody called him Caleb. He didn't mind, but then again, he wondered about Henry, who had the same familiarity in town but was never addressed as anything but Doctor. Maybe it was the age difference; more age equaled more respect. Or maybe the town still saw him as Martha and Tom's embarrassment. Well, that was Marrell, wasn't it?

"Headed home?" Leanne asked, catching up with Caleb in the parking lot.

He drew in a deep breath, promised himself he would be civil, and caught himself being fascinated by the way the late-day sun danced with the auburn of her hair. *Too* fascinated. He immediately went into standoff mode. Took a step back from her. "Going to go get Matthew first. My folks watch him during the day," he said, forcing his stare to the black asphalt beneath his feet, a much safer place to stare.

"Any plans for dinner? Because Dad and Dora have been fishing all afternoon again, and since you turned me down for the last fish fry, I thought the two of you might like to join us."

It was a tempting offer, and he appreciated that Leanne hadn't been so put off by him the other day that she was extending this invitation, but he still wasn't easy with it. He'd never been one to give much credence to people who claimed they needed closure, but he wondered if he, himself, had needed it all those years ago. Or even now? "Thanks, but Matthew's practice…"

"You've got to eat, Caleb. Couldn't he take a break for an hour or so, and the two of you come to the house? I mean, I don't know what happened between us the other day, but I'd like to have the chance to start over, on a better footing."

He cleared his throat. "Sorry about that. I'm not usually that rude."

"I don't remember you ever being rude."

He smiled, forcing himself to relax. No, he hadn't been. Not up until the very end. More like he'd always been unsuspecting. Until he'd snapped. "Oh, I'm sure I had my moments. You probably weren't there to see them, though."

"We all have our moments, don't we? Good, bad, somewhere in between, all subject to rising up and taking over without notice."

Caleb laughed. "Some of us more than others."

"Well, it's forgotten. Or, better, you owe me one. Next time I have my *moment*, you'll be cordial about it and maybe invite *me* to a fish fry."

She reached out and laid her hand on his arm, a simple, casual gesture that caused a spark to run the whole way up to his shoulder. "Maybe we *will* stop by for a little while after all," he said, wondering why the tingle was still lingering. Wondering why he liked her, even though he didn't want to. Liked her sensibilities. Saw a depth in her he'd never seen before. "So, what time do you want us?"

"About seven. Will that give Matthew enough time to get some practicing in? I figured that by the time you picked him up and got him home..."

He was pleased that she'd thought to schedule around his son's habits. It improved her status with him a little more. Something else he didn't want to happen. But, despite it all, Leanne *was* happening to him. Again. Only this time he was older. And warned. "That'll give him an hour and a half, which isn't enough, but he'll have to deal with it."

"Then we'll see you at seven," she said, giving his arm a final squeeze before she trotted off to her car.

He watched her for a moment, still curious about the tingle she'd caused in him. He remembered it from all those years ago—every time she'd touched him…although always casually. "Damn," he muttered, willing himself not to watch her. Not to take in her curves, notice her gentle bounce as she walked. But he couldn't. She'd always been the prettiest girl in Marrell. And now she was stunning. Something way beyond pretty. Yet something he wasn't going to get caught up in, again. He'd done that once and, and no matter what your age—young, old, somewhere in between—being played with hurt. Leanne had played hard with his life once, and he wasn't going to let her get close enough to do it again.

"It's so nice meeting you, Matthew," Leanne said, bending down to greet the boy. He looked just like Caleb, except where Caleb's hair was more of a sandy blond, Matthew was a definite towhead. But they had the same blue eyes, and Matthew especially had the same shy smile she remembered on Caleb years ago.

"Do you have a piano here?" the boy responded, looking around to see if he could spot one.

Caleb stepped up and put his arm around Matthew's shoulder. "When he gets fixed on something, he has a one-track mind. Right now, he's fixed on learning that Chopin piece I mentioned. It's a little above his skill level just yet, but he's working hard on it."

"The 'Fantaisie-Impromptu,'" Matthew said in a little-boy, matter-of-fact voice. "Do you know it?" he asked Leanne.

"I'm afraid I don't," she said, smiling. "But I'd love to hear you play it sometime."

"Maybe. But it's not ready yet," Matthew went on to explain. "That's why I needed to practice more tonight."

She noticed how serious he was, particularly for his young age, and wondered if he ever let himself be just a child. Go outside and play. Go wading in the creek. Play video games. Or even talk like a boy his age would talk instead of trying to sound like an adult. The way Caleb had when he was that age. "Well, I'm glad you were able to take a little time off, because we have lots of rainbow trout frying, and we're going to need help eating it all."

"Broiled is better," Matthew informed her,

folding his arms across his chest and looking up at her. "Healthier."

Caleb cleared his throat. "Matthew," he said, "watch your manners."

"I will," the child murmured, taking a step back from Leanne. "Sorry."

"That's OK," Leanne said. "Broiled is healthier, but sometimes fried is just plain good." She smiled at Caleb. "But if Matthew would prefer I broil him a piece, I can do that."

Caleb shook his head. "Part of the burden of being Matthew is knowing when to be part of the crowd. Isn't that right, son?"

Matthew nodded reluctantly. "Sorry," he conceded again, looking up at his dad and frowning. "I like fried, too."

"Would you like to go out back and watch my dad do the cooking?" she asked Matthew, realizing he was probably bored to death. He was a little boy with a lot on his mind, and it showed on his face. Same serious expression she remembered on Caleb's face back in the day.

"I'm sure my dad would like the company."

After Matthew scampered off, she turned to

Caleb, led him through the cabin to the porch and said, "He's a genius like you were at that age, isn't he?"

"Prodigy and genius…sometimes I think it's too much intellect for someone so young to handle," he replied. "Because he doesn't find much joy in being a little boy."

"Did you? Because you were that way, too," she said. "I always remember being in awe of how smart you were. It was like there wasn't anything you didn't know." They took a seat side by side on the porch swing, the way they'd sat when they'd been kids. Same memory almost. Same swing. Except they weren't swinging, and Caleb looked pathetically uncomfortable. A leftover from the past, she supposed, thinking back to that night he'd been arrested, and the look on his face when he'd been taken away. A look that had broken her heart then, and still did now when she recalled it.

"I had fun. Maybe not the way most people would define fun, especially when you're that age, but it was OK. Although that level of intellect has its burdens, which is why I worry so much about Matthew. I want him to learn from what I went through, so it doesn't have to be so rough on him. But there's that part of me that keeps saying experience is the best teacher, so I'm always walking a fine line with him." His hand accidentally brushed against her and he immediately recoiled, then moved as far away from her as he could, until he was pressed tight to the side of the swing. "So far, it's working pretty well."

"He seems happy and well-adjusted," Leanne added, wondering if Caleb would be more comfortable if she sat on the chair across from the swing. Also wondering why he didn't make that move himself since he obviously didn't want to be so close to her. But she wasn't going to say anything. Wasn't going to make the suggestion. It was Caleb's problem to deal with, if he wanted to. "So, is it tough raising him alone?"

"Sometimes. He really doesn't demand much, but there are so many times I just want him to be a little boy. I'd love to play ball with him or the two of us go for a hike in the woods. But he's never interested. Always refuses when I ask, and

I won't argue with him about it or force him to do something he doesn't want to, as there's no balance in that, and all I want to do for him is give him a balanced life. One where he knows his choices count, too. I'm sure some parents might force the issue, but I have to take particular care to nurture his abilities, and if he's happiest practicing or reading—another favorite activity of his—then I support him in that."

"Which means no baseball?"

"Not for now," Caleb said, his face so serious it looked almost ominous. "But, as staunch as he is in his likes and dislikes, he's also flexible, if I can convince him there's a reason to be. So, I keep my fingers crossed."

Leanne sighed. This was tough. Sitting here with Caleb, trying to be friendly, not sure if he wanted that. But it wasn't her nature to quit. And she did want to be friends with him again, especially if he ended up running the hospital for her. "What does his pediatrician say?"

"That I should let Matthew develop on his own course. And I agree. That's what every child needs."

It seemed like Caleb was doing everything right with Matthew, but she wondered if his plan was too well-thought-out. No room for spontaneity. Maybe because that child prodigy genius was still alive in him somewhere? Still hiding behind his proclivity for reading professional medical texts. Still being smarter than everyone else and trying to hide it. She smiled, recalling the human skeleton he'd built with sticks when he'd been, what? Seven or eight? Anatomically correct, her dad had said. "Well, how about the three of us guiding a course up to Eagle Pointe on Saturday? Pack a picnic, take some photos, let Matthew look at all the spectacular trees and plants along the way." She wasn't sure where the invitation had come from, but suddenly it seemed like a good idea, trying to reconnect with some of her past. Some of Caleb's past, too. Because so much of it was vague now. Faded from memory. Too far gone to be pulled back without some effort. And Eagle Pointe was that first effort.

"Can't," Caleb said, finally getting up from the swing. "I have work to do at the cabin, and Matthew usually spends the entire day practicing."

She was disappointed by his rejection yet, rather than dwelling on it, she, too, jumped up from the swing, but so hard it went crashing into the cabin behind her. Then she spun around and headed off around the side of the house, where her dad, Dora and Matthew were engaged in a lively discussion about Mozart. It surprised her that her dad even knew about Mozart, but he did...at least enough to keep Matthew engaged, and he seemed to be enjoying it. Something he'd rarely ever done with her.

"Let's just say that I'm not ingratiating myself with the woman who's going to be my new boss." Caleb took a blueberry muffin from the basket in the center of the kitchen table, split it in half and slathered butter on it. Real, homemade butter. Nothing better in the world. One of the fond memories from his childhood in Marrell. One of a few others that had come back to him. Playing by the river, hiking the trails, camping out on the mountain, horseback riding on old man Hendrickson's ranch. Memories that reminded him that his years here hadn't all been as bad as he'd let them become over time.

"Are you still carrying some leftover hostilities...or *other* feelings for her?" Martha Carsten asked as she poured him a cup of coffee.

"I don't know. Maybe..." he said. "But there's something about her—I don't even know how to explain it other than to say I shouldn't like her, but I think I do."

"You always did have a soft spot for her. Too big a one, as far as I'm concerned."

"But people change. I think Leanne might have. At least, she's trying hard to be nice."

"And you're falling for it again?"

"No, I'm not falling for anything. I'm just saying that she's not the same person she used to be."

"Well, just be careful that you don't get yourself so caught up in what you want her to be, the way you did before, that you can't enjoy the good life you have now," Martha said, taking a seat across from her son. Matthew was taking his morning walk with Tom, Caleb's father, so it was just the two of them in the house presently—

Caleb and his ever-outspoken mother. "She almost ruined you once, Caleb, and you, better than anybody, know how easily that happened. This time, just be careful. You've got Matthew to think about now."

"He's *all* I think about. Which is why I'm back in Marrell. He needs to be here."

"And you don't?" his mother asked, raising skeptical eyebrows.

"Other than making the best life possible for Matthew, I have no idea what else I need. Guess I'll find out, though, if I stay here." It had been a long time since he'd put his own needs first, and trying to figure out what they were wasn't easy.

"Well, whatever you do, don't let yourself down. I've always felt bad about what happened to you, felt like your father and I let you down in some way. You deserved better than you got, but I'm not sure you ever thought that then. Not sure you do now."

"What I got was the proper punishment for the crime I committed. I vandalized pretty much every building on Main Street and I'm not bitter about being punished, because I did deserve it.

I was headed down a bad path, and that year in juvenile detention is probably what saved me." He reached across the table and squeezed his mother's hand. "It wasn't your fault, or Dad's. Probably not even Leanne's, when you get down to it, since I'm the one who made the choices."

"But she hurt you, Caleb. She ridiculed you. And that business in the cave…"

"She did. But I should have been smarter." He chuckled bitterly. "For a genius, I was pretty stupid." Funny how hindsight made things clear in a way he could have never understood when he'd been a teen. It didn't erase the memories; didn't cure the pain he'd suffered. But it did make it easier to get on with it now.

"But I think you hurt more than you ever let on. I mean, I've always regretted we couldn't give you all the things your friends had. That you didn't have the nicest clothes, or the money to just go out with your friends when they wanted to buy a pizza. That's always bothered me, Caleb. But we were so poor back then…" Her voice strangled on a soft sob.

"You gave me the important things, Mom.

When I was young, I couldn't see that, but the truth is, it wasn't just about the way I dressed. It was about the way I was, and there was nothing you could do about that. And now, for me, it's all about Matthew, and making his childhood easier than mine was. If Schilling accepts him he'll be in a peer group of kids like he is, and that's what he needs."

"But what about you? Are you going to be able to work with Leanne, considering the way things were between you? Because you had no common sense when it came to that girl. Always let her walk all over you, then turned around and went back for more. I don't want to see that happen again."

"Well, to begin with, I'm a few years older, a whole lot wiser, and I have other more important things to do in my life. So, there's no need to worry about me reverting back to my teen years." He shook his head. "Something about getting married, getting wounded and raising a kid changes things." Popping a bit of muffin into his mouth, he chewed, swallowed, then continued. "And Leanne isn't on my radar now. She's just…well, I was going to say a colleague, but she's really my new boss."

"Can you deal with that, Caleb? Be honest with yourself. Can you deal with having her in your life again?"

"If I stay here, I'll have to." Pragmatic thinking. But could it really work out? Honestly, he didn't know. "Anyway, don't worry about me. I've faced worse than Leanne and come out OK."

"You always come out OK." She took another sip of coffee. "But, whatever the case, I think you need more adult companionship. You're a great doctor, a devoted dad, but where, in there, is something for you? I think you've gotten into such a habit of putting everything and everyone ahead of you, I'm not sure you could find yourself in that mess. It worries me, Caleb. *You* concern me."

"I'm doing fine, Mom. Glad to be here…with an adult perspective this time. And I hope it works out that we can stay." He did, because he wanted stability. Not only for Matthew, but for himself. He'd been too long without it, and the older he got, the more he craved it.

"I do, too," she said, taking hold of the coffee-pot and refreshing his cup. "Because where better than home?"

Where better, indeed.

"And in the meantime, you know that trip up to Eagle Pointe with Leanne that you turned down..."

"How did you know about that?" Stupid question. This was a small town. People knew everything about everybody. Always had, always would.

"Henry mentioned it when I saw him at the grocery this morning. He said Leanne's going up there anyway, and that I should try to convince you to go with her because you're really very rigid and the hike might do you some good."

"I'd thought about taking Matthew up there, sooner or later. Just hadn't planned on it being with Leanne."

"Well, if she's really going to be your boss, then I suppose you've got to put it behind you at some point. Just sayin'..." She gave her son a wink. "Anyway, you used to hate Marrell. Are you liking it any better now that you're back?"

He tapped his temple. "Different perspective this time. You know, the whole older and wiser thing."

"Being a parent does that to you. Makes you look at the world in a totally different way. Including moving back to a place you swore you'd never move back to."

"Well, apart from just working at the hospital, Leanne did ask me to run it once Henry retires. I guess if I take the job, that's looking at the world in a totally different way."

"Henry did mention she wants to get back to her life in Seattle. I think there may be a fiancé, or something. So, are you going to take it?"

Leanne engaged? She'd hinted at it, but hearing it said aloud…he wasn't quite able to wrap his head around it. Didn't want to know why. Didn't want to think about why he didn't want to know. But, one way or another, whatever Leanne did wasn't going to change his plans, and he wasn't going to let it bother him. But it did, over the next few hours. Took up more space in his mind than it should. And he had no idea why.

CHAPTER THREE

"I'M GLAD YOU decided to come up with me today," Leanne told Caleb. They were approaching the trailhead, Leanne in the lead, Caleb bringing up the rear so he could keep an eye on Matthew, who was wandering from side to side on the trail, showing as little interest as possible in everything. "I think Matthew will enjoy this," she said.

Caleb gave his son a dubious glance. "I hope so. As often as not, though, I have no idea what Matthew will enjoy until I see him enjoying something. It makes me feel like I'm not being a good dad because he keeps to his own little world so much of the time, and won't let anybody else...*me* in. I hate seeing how isolated he is, but this will be good because he doesn't ever go outside, unless he has to."

Leanne stopped on the trail, and turned to face

him. "You haven't brought him up here yet?" The hike to the top was remote, but not too rugged. Not totally isolated from the world, the top of the point—their destination—overlooked a magnificent valley opening onto the river where she'd spent so many great days rafting, kayaking and hiking. And taking pictures. She'd loved taking pictures. All in all, Eagle Pointe was a beautiful place from her childhood, and she had many cherished memories of the great times she'd had there with her friends. "Because we used to come here all the time, and I'd just assumed this would be one of the first places you'd want to show him."

"Eagle Pointe doesn't really hold any great memories for me and, to be honest, I hadn't given it a lot of thought until you mentioned it."

"Well, I'm glad you changed your mind. Maybe you can start some new memories up there today." She turned back around then scrambled over a jagged rock in the path, before she plopped down on a fallen pine-tree trunk to tie her boot. "Memories for you and Matthew," she said, looking up at him.

Memories she didn't have with her own dad because he'd always been too busy to make them with her.

"Making memories is one of the reasons I want to get us established here. Vegas is a confining place to raise a kid, and it's pretty confining for an adult if you're not big into the social life. Which I'm not...anymore."

"Anymore?" she asked, grinning.

"Let's just say there was a time when I was a lot more social than I am now." He shrugged. "The weight of adult responsibility slammed down hard on me."

"It slams down on all of us, to some degree. Some more than others, it seems," Leanne said. "I'm sorry."

"Not complaining. Just finding it difficult to adjust my coping skills every day or so."

Leanne laughed. "Well, if you find a solution for that, patent it, sell it and retire a rich man, because I think what you described fits all of us. As they say in today's vernacular, *adulting* isn't always easy."

"Well, I got my crash course when I became a

single dad and, so far, I've barely even cracked the spine on *that* book."

"Yeah, but look at you. Real dad. From what I'm gathering, a very good dad, which makes you a good man. Sounds to me like you're doing fine on your own, without the book."

She tilted back a water flask, took a drink, and extended it to offer Caleb a drink, but he refused. So, she capped it and put it back into her backpack. "I hated this place. Absolutely hated it. Not Eagle Pointe, but Marrell. Couldn't wait to get out of here. In fact, everything I did when I was a kid was in preparation for leaving."

"As I seem to recall..." he said, his voice trailing off to some distant memory. "Remember when I took Mrs. Jenkins's classic T-Bird, just so we could run away? We were, what? Thirteen? Didn't even know how to drive but we were on our way, for about three blocks. Then I got a three-month sentence to pick up trash on the streets. Nice dream..."

She chuckled. "Yeah, well...we tried. That counts, right?"

"And here you are, back again and still looking for a way to get out."

"But I'm here with a purpose."

"Yeah, to convince me to run the hospital, *then* leave."

She laughed, squinted up at the sun, stood up from the old log on which she'd been sitting, and dusted off the seat of her pants. "A girl's got to do what a girl's got to do. Anyway, to sweeten the deal about you staying, I made you pimiento sandwiches, hoping it's a bribe that'll work, because your mom told me they're your favorite."

He chuckled. "That's what she always thought was my favorite. Truth was, I used to take them down to the river and use the cheese as bait when I fished."

"Well, no fishing today, so I guess you're going to have to eat your bait. Oh, but peanut butter and grape jam for Matthew and me. Because that cheese…" She turned up her nose and shook her head. "I don't think so."

"We could take that cheese out to the dump later, then watch and see if the bears come out and take it."

Leanne grabbed up her backpack and slung it over her shoulder. "Not even the bears, Caleb." Then started off toward the next level of the trail, where it went from flat walking to a more elevated hike. When she got to the trailhead, though, she paused, pulled a floppy, cloth hat from her pocket and put it on her head, ready to move. But looked long and hard at the trail up ahead of her as a peculiar jitteriness overtook her. A lump formed in the pit of her stomach and she swallowed hard, redoubled her concentration and focused on the little chickadee sitting on a maple bough just off the trail, looking at her.

Why the sudden apprehension? Or the onset of jitters? It didn't make sense.

"You OK?" he asked, stepping up next to her.

She blew out a long breath and nodded. "Yep," she lied, when everything inside her was screaming for her to turn around and run away. She didn't know why, couldn't dredge up a memory that should elicit such a response, so she chalked it up to being tired. Too much work lately. Too much Eric. Not enough time for herself. Yes, that's what it had to be. She was simply tired, and this long hike reminded her just how much. "Anyway, are you ready to get on? We're only about halfway to the top, and Matthew looks like he's ready to move."

"When can we go home so I can practice?" Matthew asked, when he noticed they were looking at him.

Leanne laughed. "No practicing for a while. Today's your day off."

"I don't take days off," he said. "My fingers don't feel right if I don't practice."

"Well, could you practice on something else today?"

"They have a piano where we're going?" he asked hopefully.

"No piano, I'm afraid, but lots of trees and flowers. And *big* rocks you can climb on. If we're lucky, we'll find an eagle's nest, too."

"How am I supposed to practice on all of that?" he asked, his face drawing into a definite pout, his voice taking on the sharp edge that reminded her so much of Caleb as he was now, *not* back then.

"With this." She fished an old digital camera

from her pocket and handed it to him. "Have you ever used a camera?" she asked, knowing that these days people were more inclined to use their phones to take photos. But Matthew didn't have a phone. She'd asked Martha about that yesterday, after Caleb had agreed to come with her, then spent the next couple of hours trying to roust out her old camera, the one she'd used up here so many times.

"No," he said, taking hold of the camera and looking at it curiously. "What does it do?"

"It takes pictures of the things you want to remember."

"Like Dad's phone," he said, not really interested yet.

"Only better."

That caught his attention. "Could it take pictures of my music?" he asked.

"It can. Or that tree over there." She pointed to a massive ponderosa pine just off the trail. Standing nearly eighty feet tall, its trunk was straight, its bark a beautiful cinnamon brown, and its seven-inch green needles splayed magnificently in perfect symmetry. She recalled the tree from her childhood. Remembered picnicking and reading books under it and, yes, even smooching with her boyfriend *du jour* there. To her, this tree had always represented the beginning of wonderful adventures, a place where exciting things started to unfold and, for some reason, she wanted Matthew to like it every bit as much as she did. Had she and Caleb ever connected in some way under that tree…another picnic, a chat?

She didn't remember, and she should have, because other memories were there. Just none of him, and it was beginning to make her wonder why Caleb hadn't resonated more. He should have. She'd had such a crush at a young age, and more about him *should* have registered. Didn't understand why it hadn't. "You can take a picture of that tree, Matthew."

He looked mildly interested. "How?" he asked.

Leanne bent down alongside him, showed him how to place the camera in its proper position, explained that what he could see in its viewer was what would be on the picture, then instructed him to click. He did, several times.

Then held the camera out in front of him and looked up at Leanne. "When can I see the pictures?" he asked.

"Now, on the view screen. And when you get home, your daddy can hook it up to the computer and save them, so you can look at them anytime." She showed him how to flip through the pictures he'd just taken, then stood back and watched his face as he did so.

"Amazing," Caleb said quietly, as Matthew flipped through a couple times, then settled on his favorite to show his dad.

"Do you like this one?" he asked Caleb.

It was a close-up of the tree's trunk, showing fine detailing in the bark. A very complicated composition, all things considered, and a very thoughtful one that focused on one little beetle scurrying its way up the tree, probably disturbed by all the attention Matthew was giving it. "Very much," Caleb answered. "You did a good job."

"Can I take more pictures on the hike, Daddy?" he asked, finally sounding interested in something for the first time since they'd gotten here.

"You'll have to ask Leanne. It's her camera."

He put on a smile for Matthew, but the instant Matthew turned away to take another picture, Caleb's face scrunched into a scowl. Not a deep one, but one that indicated he was uncomfortable with something.

Leanne studied the scowl on Caleb's face for a moment. Wondered if she was responsible for it. Was it about her and Matthew? Or the job she'd offered him? Marrell, in general? Perhaps something she knew nothing about? It bothered her, but she wasn't in a place to ask. Her memory of Caleb was so scattered, so broken. Bits and pieces of a jigsaw childhood that, she was sure, no longer belonged to this man here. Well, no matter what it was, she was determined not to ruin this for Matthew. He was *finally* having fun, and she wanted to keep it that way. "No, it's Matthew's camera. And he can take as many pictures with it as he wants. It has brand-new batteries and a sizable memory card, so he should be good to go for quite a while."

"I appreciate that," Caleb said, again forcing a smile to his face.

"Me, too," Matthew said, then shyly stepped up to Leanne and gave her a hug around the waist.

Even though Matthew's intellect and talents were off the charts, for this moment right now he was an average little boy discovering new things and having fun with them. Being part of that was…different. Exciting. Surprisingly, while she'd always been indifferent to kids on a personal level, she was really liking this. "You've got to promise me, Matthew, that once you've got all of today's photos downloaded to your computer, you'll ask me over to see them."

"I will," he said solemnly. "And Daddy will cook dinner. He's really good at chicken. But he always serves peas with it, and I don't like peas."

Leanne laughed, smiled and winked at Caleb. "That would be great. Chicken and, well…no peas. If it's OK with your daddy."

Caleb smiled back, and this time it wasn't so forced. "I can cook other things, too."

"Nope," Leanne said, her grin at Caleb widening. "This is Matthew's date, and if he wants chicken without peas, that's exactly what I want." She sensed that Caleb was beginning to loosen up a little, but he was still very standoffish. This day was for him, too, and she hoped he would enjoy it. Or, parts of it.

It was an easy hike, for which he was glad because Matthew was having the best time taking photos—of everything. Rocks, dirt, logs, sky, his feet, Leanne from all angles... The camera had opened a whole new world for him, and he hadn't mentioned missing his piano once. For that, Caleb knew he owed Leanne a great big thank-you, as she'd done something for Matthew he'd rarely been able to do himself—given him the freedom to be a regular little kid for a while. He also owed her the rest of her day with a man who wasn't so held back or grumpy, the way he'd been so far. She was trying hard to have fun, to be friendly, to make the day pleasant for all of them, and he needed to do the same. "He loves that camera," Caleb said to Leanne, laying his hand on the flat of her lower back and pointing to Matthew, who ran well ahead of them on the trail, clicking away at everything in his path. "Thank you. For him. Even for me."

"It's such a simple thing. I glad he likes it."

"I am, too. Especially since he's usually resistant to trying new things."

"I think all you have to do is show him something new and prove why it will be interesting for him. Which sounds simple enough, but I'm sure is very difficult."

"The fact is, I should have known he would like photography, because he's a very observant and artistic little boy, and I didn't because I've never thought to have him take a picture."

"Maybe you just get yourself overwhelmed with the big things and miss out on all the things to see and do in smaller situations. It's easy to do. I'm like that a lot of the time back in Seattle. Too caught up in what I have to do to enjoy what I'd like to do."

"What do you like to do?" he asked.

"This. Nature. Hiking. Photography. Rock climbing. Remember how I used to love that?" None of which Eric liked or would even consider. "How Jack Hanson spent weeks teaching me?"

"Well, I'm sure there are probably a lot more things Matthew would like to do. I suppose it's up to me to find out what they are." He removed his hand from her back and stepped away when he realized just how long he'd been touching her like that. Touching her and enjoying it. And now wondering why she'd let him linger in that touch so long. "Anyway, there's still a lot more trail to cover, so I'd suggest…"

She nodded. "If we can catch up with him. I think he's completely forgotten we're here, and I'm not sure I like the idea of him getting so far ahead." Clear-cut worry spread over her face, as she ran to catch up with Matthew. Something any good mother would do. And suddenly Caleb could picture her as a mother to a child or children or… Matthew. He shook that cozy image off, and hurried to catch up to her.

"You're going to be a great mother, if you ever decide you want to have children," he said, when they were finally walking shoulder to shoulder, only a few paces behind Matthew. "I hope your fiancé can appreciate that."

"My fiancé?" She looked up to face him. "Where'd you hear that?"

"My mother. Plus, you dropped some hints."

Without missing a beat, and maybe too quickly, she said, "Didn't mean to drop hints because he's not my fiancé. More like we're just calling it a committed relationship for now. Trying to see where it goes."

"I thought that's one of the reasons you wanted to get back to Seattle right away."

"It's on the list, and we're definitely working toward that outcome, but the real reason I want to get back is because I have a life there. Not here. I've worked hard to get it and I'm not in any particular hurry to change it."

She seemed almost agitated now. Something about Seattle? Or the man with whom she was involved? "Am I going places I shouldn't with this conversation?" he asked.

She frowned, pushed her cap back off her face. "Not really. I'm just under some pressure right now. Nothing big. But I've got decisions…" She stopped.

"Like whether or not you want to come home to Marrell?"

"No. That's not one of them. Especially if you accept my offer. But my job is changing, and

my life is changing… Eric is the first relationship I've had in so long I can't even remember,
and it's…complicated. Right now, everything's
complicated. But like I said, I'm going back to
Seattle and things will even out once I'm there.
The sooner, the better.

"Because besides wanting *my* life back, I want
you to make your mark here, Caleb. I want you to
be the future of Sinclair Hospital, if that's what
you want to be. So, I'm not going to be stepping
all over your toes trying to prevent you from having something I really want you to have. *If you
want it.* So, do you?"

"Well, that was straight to the point." Leanne
certainly didn't sound like the self-centered, un-
thoughtful girl she used to be. In fact, she seemed
quite the opposite. Which he liked. "So, my answer is—if Matthew is accepted into Schilling's
school, yes. You've got me because, in the long
run, I'm not sure how well my shoulder's going
to hold up, and this will be a good decision for
me because of that. But if he isn't accepted…"
He shrugged, then glanced up the trail at Matthew, who was breaking away again and now

veering a little too far off the path to take his photos. "Matthew, buddy. Back on the trail. Stay where I can see you."

Matthew's response was to turn around and snap a picture of Leanne and Caleb, who were still walking shoulder to shoulder up the trail, their hands brushing casually against each other as they moved, and looking almost like a real, connected couple. "Save it for the eagle's nest." He pointed to the top of the tree just beyond where Matthew was standing. It was sitting near the top, nestled down into the branches of a pine tree, precariously perched and leaning just barely above the cliff line. "See it, buddy? Right in front of you. Look up, but don't go any closer to the edge." He hurried to catch up to Matthew to make sure his son didn't go any farther because straight down...the ledge, *the cave*.

"I wish there was an eagle in it for him," Leanne said, stopping to shift her backpack.

"I'm sure we'll be back and eventually he'll find his eagle." Caleb stopped next to Matthew and reached out to keep a steadying hand on him. "Once Matthew feels comfortable doing something, he's good to go anytime, and I think he's comfortable with his hike." He smiled down at his son. "You do like this, don't you, buddy?"

Matthew nodded, but didn't take his focus, or his camera, off the eagle's nest.

"Well, let's hope Schilling accepts him and the two of you can stay here. And that's purely selfish, because you're my short list, Caleb. Nobody else on it. Anyway, once Matthew gets finished taking pictures of the nest, could I interest you in a pimiento cheese sandwich?"

"If you insist," he said, laughing as he turned up his nose. Wondering why he was vowing nothing personal with her yet standing right smack on the edge of it. *Again.* And having a good time. What the hell was he thinking?

She thought about the casual touches. Caleb's hand on her back. Brushing up against him, or him brushing up against her. The way he'd taken her hand to help her up a rock where she didn't have a good foothold. The way he'd put his arm around her shoulders when they'd stood together and looked out over the river down below. They fit, even though they were all just instinctual, polite gestures. But she hadn't objected, because she liked the way they'd felt. The way *she* felt when he touched her. It wasn't the way she'd felt when Eric touched her. He'd always had an intent behind his touches. It was like he'd calculated them. Penciled them in on his calendar. Time to hold Leanne's hand. Time to put an arm around her shoulders. That's the way Eric was, of course, and she was used to it. But Caleb's touch...natural. Spontaneous. And nice.

The day had played out quite well, and she was glad Caleb had eventually loosened up and enjoyed himself. He was so lovely to be with when he was in a good mood, and his good mood had permeated the entire afternoon. After he'd choked down half a pimiento sandwich, trying to be a good sport, then switched over to a peanut butter and jam, they'd climbed rocks, posed about a million times for Matthew to take pictures, gone wading in a creek—so many fun things and, too soon, the day was over.

But every now and then, throughout the day, especially in the moments when she'd been alone, that lump in her stomach had tried to overtake her. She'd forced it back and kept herself in the moment, which, as it turned out, had always been a good moment. But it her worried because she knew it for what it was—anxiety. Caused by what, she didn't know. But what she did know was that she'd suffered a mighty high dose of it several times over the day.

"I think we did him in," she said, when Matthew finally gave up and let Caleb carry him the rest of the way back down the trail.

"I think we about did me in, too," he replied, as Leanne took his backpack to relieve him of a little of the load. "I don't remember it being so...steep."

She laughed. "You didn't even go all the way up to the steep part." Up where the craggy rocks broke off into nothing, and the only thing to catch you if you fell over was the thin lip of Devil's Cave. Devil's Cave...a name that made her skin crawl.

"I went as far as I'd allow Matthew to go. Nobody has any business going beyond where we went."

"We used to, didn't we?"

His eyes went distant for a moment, and he sucked in a sharp breath. "We did a lot of things we shouldn't have."

She saw the look returning to his face, the one from earlier. Didn't know what to make of it, so she simply ignored it because she wanted their day to end on a good note and not on the one that was brewing again in Caleb. "Did you enjoy today, because at first…?"

He blinked hard, cleared his throat, and visibly forced a smile back to his face. "At first, I didn't. But I got over it, especially when I saw how much Matthew was enjoying himself and how much you'd put into us having a good time. Sometimes I…" He shrugged. "Sometimes I get in my own way, as my mother has said."

"Well, I'm glad you eventually stepped out of your way, if not for yourself then for Matthew."

"And for you, too. Look, it's been a good day, Leanne. Thank you for inviting me, and next time I'll try to do better from the start." They reached his truck, where he placed his son in the passenger's seat, then turned to face Leanne, reached out and brushed her cheek. He stood there for a moment, looking into her eyes, before he finally walked around to his side of the truck and opened the door to climb in. "I'd do this again, if you'd ask me," he said.

If *she* asked *him*. But would *he* ask *her*? It was the question playing in her mind when he drove off, leaving her standing there in the middle of a pack of late-in-the-day hikers, watching the cloud of dust he left in his wake. That was a very good question. *Would he ask her?* She wasn't sure why that seemed so important, but it did.

"It *was* a nice day," Leanne said to herself a little while later, as she sat alone on her dad's front porch, just drinking in the peacefulness of the night. Her dad and Dora were at Red's Saloon in town, probably dancing the night away, and she was grateful for the time alone. Grateful to reflect on her life ahead, without someone interrupting her or offering an opinion.

Where would she be a month from now? Or a year? She wondered about that from time to time, because she loved her job, loved her clinic.

Couldn't foresee changes, but didn't necessarily rule them out either. Which made her question this niggling little bit of restlessness that seemed to be popping up. What was that about? Because two weeks ago she didn't want to leave Seattle, ever. Then a few days ago the idea that she could have a different life had wiggled its way in and she hadn't squeezed it back out. "Just getting nostalgic," she said, glancing at the clock on her phone, knowing she wasn't the nostalgic type about anything. "OK, Eric…"

He hadn't called yet, but he would. He was dependable like that, unless there was a medical emergency. Yes, Eric… It wasn't really a limbo relationship. She spent three or four nights a week at his apartment. They ate together that often. Usually set aside one day of their weekend to be with each other. She shut her eyes to picture him, but the first image to pop up was Caleb, with the smudge of dirt he'd had on his face earlier when they'd climbed up Big Rock. Eric was never smudged. He was fussy. Never a hair out of place. Never a wrinkle in his clothes, the way Caleb's cotton cowboy shirt had been a mass of wrinkles. Never dust on his boots, the way Caleb's had been nothing but dust. Not that Eric ever wore boots.

"Stop," she said aloud, giving herself a physical shake to get rid of the mental picture of the two of them standing side by side. Why this stupid comparison? She was with Eric, not Caleb. Yet Caleb was taking up much more mental space than Eric right now. And despite his sometimes-god-awful attitude, she liked him. Saw something in him she couldn't define. Maybe didn't understand. But something...

Shaking both men out of her head, she absently punched in Eric's number, waited for him to pick up and, for no reason that made good sense, almost hoped he wouldn't. He didn't belong here. Not in this place. Not in her thoughts. Nothing about him did. And right now, even thinking about his voice seemed intrusive. So much so she almost hung up after the second ring, but...

"Yes?" came the familiar voice on the other end of the call. His generic greeting irritated her, even though that's how he always answered the phone, knowing it was her.

"Yes? Can't you do better than that?" she said, trying hard not to snap.

"Something wrong?" he asked.

"No," she said, wondering about the thin, raw nerve that was causing her to ball her fists. "Just a little too much Montana, I think." She blew out a cleansing breath, and relaxed back into the porch swing. "Anyway, you're probably working and I interrupted you. Right?"

"Actually, I'm getting ready to go home, kick back, look at your picture and wish you were here. So, how was your day?"

It was nothing she wanted to talk about. At least, not to Eric. "Nothing special." OK, that was a lie. There was a lot more to it, but Eric didn't need to know that. Particularly since she didn't understand why simply talking to him was making her feel on edge this evening.

"Sounds boring."

"Not really. I took a walk, saw some old sights." And hadn't realized how nice her day with Caleb had been until it had ended.

"Boring," he repeated. "Now, tell me something I want to hear. Talk sexy to me."

Yeah, right. Like she was in the mood for *that*. "How about I talk prednisone to you, because I just read that…"

To each his own, she thought several minutes later, after they'd hung up on a very unsatisfactory conversation. They hadn't connected on any level. She hadn't even wanted to try, deferring instead to a discussion on a common medicine, and she knew she owed him better. At least an expression of affection in her good-night to him, rather than the generic "Talk to you tomorrow" she'd signed off with.

Sighing, she looked at Eric's picture on her phone, hoping to spark something in her, yet still not feeling anything. She wanted to. Knew she should. But tonight…she was in a strange mood. Didn't understand it, couldn't explain it, but she thought she should put it right with Eric before she wandered off to bed, because she was sure he'd heard the discontent in her voice.

Yet she just didn't want to engage with him again. Or explain her mood, which he'd insist on. Or deal with anything. So, she decided to take the impersonal way out and punched in to text him good-night, rather than call him.

She got half of a half-hearted message typed before she was interrupted by a text from him. Had he felt the same ho-hum feeling she had? The distance?

Feeling a little better that she'd have another chance to get it right, Leanne pressed the icon to open the message.

I miss you.

So sweet, she thought.

Want to spend more time with you.

And she wanted to spend more time with him. Wanted to get the old feeling back.

I can be there in ten minutes, so get naked and wait for me. Since she's not here we've got the whole night to play. And I've got some new games for you! Now, get ready to talk sexy to me.

CHAPTER FOUR

TALK SEXY TO HIM? Who? A girlfriend? Eric had a girlfriend other than her? Was he telling *her* he loved her, the way he told her?

"Talk sexy to you, my…"

The first hour post-text, Leanne sat in a stupor, still on her dad's front porch, not sure what to do, what to think, how to react. This was Eric. The man who'd wanted to make their relationship exclusive from the start of it. The man who'd suggested they move in together when she returned from Marrell. Eric, the cheating, no-good—

…get naked and wait for me. Since she's not here we've got the whole night to play.

Since when had Eric had a whole night to do anything other than sleep? *And play?* Eric didn't play. Not ever. He was straightforward in, well, everything in his life. Everything! "Damn it," she muttered, rereading his text for at least the one-hundredth time. So, all these nights when he claimed he was working late, was he really playing? All those weekends when he'd been called in unexpectedly, had he been off somewhere, getting naked? Being unexclusive? *Hearing sexy talk?*

Leanne blew out a frustrated breath and rubbed at the dull throb setting in between her eyes. She couldn't even fathom this, yet it was as obvious as the coyote howling in the distance. The sound pierced her ears just as the images of Eric and this other woman pierced her thoughts. She'd been cheated on. And lied to. But how had she been so gullible? How could she have not seen it? Or sensed it? Or suspected it?

He'd said that once she got the situation with Sinclair Hospital straightened out, they had some serious talking to do, and she'd assumed that meant marriage, which, before now, had only been a hint. Did he really intend asking her to marry him when he couldn't even be faithful to her during their courtship? And was it true what they said: once a cheater, always a cheater? Had they gone any further, which they would not do now, would he have cheated all through it? "Seriously, Eric, you lying—"

Why wasn't she crying about this? Or, not even close to it? So far, only anger. White-hot, searing anger that made her want to scream. She should have wanted tears, but they weren't in her. She should have wanted to call him to see if this had been a mistake, but she didn't want to hear his voice, didn't want to waste her time. Eric was her past now. Put there much more easily than she'd thought she could. Which meant, well...she wasn't sure what it meant. Especially since there was anger where there should have been pain.

After the initial shock of how she'd been so stupid had worn off, she felt like talking to someone. Caleb. No particular reason why him. And not that anything he could say would make much of a difference now. But she just needed...interaction. Another person there simply to reassure her that she wasn't overreacting. Or stupid. Someone to help her figure out what to do, what not to do. How to get over it, or deal with it in its initial stages. But it was going on to ten now, and while she wasn't sleeping, she was sure everybody else in Marrell was getting ready to, except for the few people who manned the hospital at night, and old man Clarence at the gas station, who stayed awake all night, waiting for pretty much nobody to stop in and fill up.

Well, she wasn't going to disturb Caleb now, since that might also disturb Matthew. And she doubted that old man Clarence would want to hear about her messed-up love life. So, the only other option... Leanne trudged up to her room, changed her clothes, and went to the hospital. Work always had a curative effect on her. It's what she knew better than anything. What she trusted more than anything.

"We weren't expecting you this time of the night, Dr. Sinclair," Marjorie Lawson said, as Leanne entered the central nursing hub. "Dr. Baily is in on call, sleeping, Dr. Mortenson is in Emergency, working on that novel of his, Dr. Carsten is with a patient, and we certainly didn't anticipate having a fourth doctor on. Especially since weekends are always slow around here."

Marjorie Lawson, like so many of the other

hospital workers, was a transplant who'd come to Marrell looking for a quieter way of life. She was charge nurse on nights, and her husband Ben was chief physical therapist. Both were valued employees at Sinclair Hospital. "Dr. Carsten is here right now?" she asked Marjorie, suddenly taking up the thought again that she wanted to talk to him.

"He came in about an hour ago. Mr. Allerd started having chest pains, and Dr. Baily was tied up delivering Ellie Harmon's baby at the time, so we called Dr. Carsten, since he was first on the list."

The hospital was eerily quiet at a time when Leanne wanted to be surrounded by noise, and activity, and anything else that would distract her. "Well, I just decided to get a jump on tomorrow," Leanne explained. "So, what room is Dr. Carsten in?"

"Two ten. Unless he's finished. If you can't find him there, you might try his office, because he said he wasn't going to go back home tonight."

Leanne nodded, debating whether she really wanted to chase down Caleb or simply leave it alone. What would she say to him anyway? And why Caleb? Why was he the one who first popped into her mind and not…well, she really didn't have any friends here anymore. So, there was no one else to talk to except her dad, who didn't listen, and Dora. And she didn't want to disturb their night. For the first time, it dawned on her how utterly alone she was in Marrell. Totally, completely alone…except for Caleb. The way it had been once, a very long time ago.

"Look, if you happen to see Dr. Carsten, would you— No, never mind. I'll take care of it myself." No, she wasn't going to do it. Wasn't going to bother him with this latest glitch in her life. She'd chosen her mess when she'd accepted her first date with Eric, thinking his reputation with the ladies was exaggerated, which, apparently, it hadn't been. And now it was hers to get over. On her own. Even though she was still very tempted to talk to Caleb.

Leanne hated being so wishy-washy. Hated that she was trying to avoid something she really should face head-on. "I'll be in my office, Marjorie. Call me if you need me." Hated her indecisiveness. But it was there, smeared all over her like a child smeared peanut butter and grape jam all over himself when he ate a PB and J sandwich.

And right now, her hospital wasn't curing a blessed thing. If anything, it was making matters worse. Because Eric worked in a hospital, and hospital equated to trust, and Eric had betrayed their trust. "Shoot," she said, slogging her way down to her office. What was she going to do?

"Leanne seemed a little off," Marjorie told Caleb, as he typed patient notes into the computer at the nursing hub. "I think she wanted to see you, but she changed her mind."

"And she didn't come in to see a patient?" he asked, wondering what Leanne was up to.

"Not that I know of. She just seemed…lost. Like she was here, but wasn't sure why."

"Well, she's got a lot on her mind." Her future, her hospital—two very big things. Who could blame her if she was distracted? "Anyway, I'll be in my office if you need me. Mr. Allerd is resting comfortably now and I'd like his vital signs checked every two hours. I'd also like someone to look in on him about every thirty minutes until I write new orders in the morning. Don't want him disturbed, though. Let him sleep through those checks, if possible."

Like any patient in any hospital ever got the opportunity to sleep through anything. Being in the hospital was the worst for someone who needed rest. Housekeeping trooping in and out, medicines distributed, vital signs checked, routine check-ins just to make sure the patient was still there, blood draws, food trays, therapists, visiting clergy, bed baths, linen changes…any number of things conspired against bed rest, all of which he'd come to know very personally when he'd been recuperating from his war wounds. All kinds of visitors, all kinds of interruptions, but never his wife. Not once.

Nancy's image popped into his mind for a second, and he blinked it away. There was nothing about her he wanted to remember. Nothing at all. But Leanne…he remembered so much. The good, especially the bad. So, what had Leanne wanted? Why was she here tonight? He wondered about it on his way down to his office. Wondered about it so much he turned right at the junction where he should have gone left to get to his office and headed toward hers. Actually, it was her dad's. They were sharing, for the time being.

"Leanne?" he whispered, poking his head through the door of the dark outer office. "You in here? It's Caleb."

No one answered, but he saw the light coming from under the door into the main office, and as he walked toward it he picked up the hum of a faint conversation coming from inside. It was Leanne. Even though her voice was soft, almost blending with the night, he recognized it. He started to step forward to knock on the door, but something stopped him as his fist was raised in midair, ready to strike the frame.

"No, Eric. I'm done," she said. "You're pathetic, a total loser, and I don't ever want to see you again."

Her words stopped him cold. What he was hearing now were almost the very same words she'd used on him that night. She'd called him pathetic. Loser. Then abandoned him to the most humiliating fate a boy his age could face.

Suddenly, the thoughts of that night stabbed him almost as sharply as the words had. He'd gone up to Eagle Pointe with a bunch of the kids, only because she'd asked him to come along. She'd never done that before. At least, not since they'd been very young. And, of course, he'd accepted. Blind faith. True love. Stupidity.

His mother had warned him but, of course, he hadn't listened. "Don't do it, Caleb. You know how she treats you *every single time.*"

He had. But that time, like every other time she'd crooked her little finger at him, he'd hoped it was going to be different. A poor, foolish, sixteen-year-old's delusion, as it had turned out. Since Leanne's *only* intention had been to humiliate him.

No, I don't want things to work, Eric.

Her words broke back into his thoughts, and he couldn't help but wonder if she was stringing this Eric along, only to snap him in two, like a brittle twig, the way she'd done to him? Had she really changed, the way he'd been convincing himself she had? Or was this the real Leanne now, and the nice one he was growing fond of was only being nice because she wanted something from him?

Caleb shuddered. He didn't want to hear any more. Couldn't think. Couldn't stomach it. So, he spun around and left the office. But tonight, he wasn't running. Wasn't crying. No, Leanne would never get him to do that again. He might remember those days, but he wasn't doomed to repeat them. Not anymore. And especially not anywhere near her.

"You're looking…somber," Leanne told Caleb while she slid down into the seat across from him in the cafeteria. He was having coffee, and the scowl on his face was so off-putting she'd debated whether she even wanted his company. But that's all she'd thought about since the whole Eric debacle—how she simply wanted to be around Caleb. Not to confide in, not to drag into the middle of her problems. Just to be around, because he had such a calming effect, the way he always had when they'd been little.

Except there was nothing calming about him now. He was like a storm cloud, getting ready to open up. The Caleb who seemed to always be lurking just behind his attempts to be nice.

She wanted the old one back. The one who, when they'd been six and she'd fallen off the swing and broken her arm, had tried to get her to stop crying by telling her that she was special because she was the only one in kindergarten who had a cast. He'd even drawn flowers on it to make her more special. And when they'd been seven and her puppy had wandered off, he'd been the one who'd searched for that puppy for hours, who'd refused to give up and go home until he'd found it. Then when they'd been eight and her grandma had died, it had been his hand she held on to throughout the entire funeral. Caleb— always Caleb. Not her dad. Not anybody else. Just Caleb Carsten, always comforting when they'd been kids yet, there was nothing comforting about him now, and that stirred something upsetting in her.

Yet still, Caleb's who she wanted tonight. But he wasn't there. He wasn't calming, wasn't even cordial, and it concerned her that *this* might be the real Caleb now. Someone who would definitely not draw flowers on her cast. "Are you OK, Caleb?" she asked, taking the plastic sippy lid off her coffee. "You seem…angry."

"I'm fine," he said, his voice brusque, his eyes unemotional.

"After we had such a nice day—I'm worried about you."

"Why? We're just associates. Not close enough to be drawn into each other's worries."

That stung. It shouldn't have, because he was right. Still, it did. "Is that how it is?"

"How's it supposed to be, Leanne? You tell me."

"Tell you what, Caleb? Tell me what to say, because I don't understand what's going on with you right now."

"Are you planning on staying here? Asking me to take over the hospital one minute, then yanking it away from me the next? Is that how this is going to work?"

"What?" She had no idea what this was about. "I asked you to take over, and that's what I want.

Nothing's changed." Or, had it? As, it seemed like it might have. At least, for Caleb. "And I don't understand why you're even asking."

"Because *you* change, Leanne. You always have. Say one thing, do another."

"Look, it's obvious you're angry with me, but I don't know what I've done. Don't know why I've given you the impression that I'm going back on my offer. You're the *only* one I want to head my hospital, and I haven't even considered another possibility."

"Not even yourself?"

"I told you Caleb, *I don't want it.*" Now she was getting angry. "I don't want to step into admin work, don't want to stay in Marrell. So why are you doubting me? Why are we always doing this dance routine where I get backed into the corner? I'm trying really hard to be your friend, and Matthew's friend, yet…" She tossed her hands in the air in exasperation. "Why are you acting like this?"

"Because you made another one of your *changes*, and I thought you might change your mind about the hospital, as well."

She shut her eyes and rubbed her forehead. "What *change*?" Not only did she not understand, this conversation was so bizarre it bothered her. And she really wasn't in the mood to deal with it, considering what she'd just gone through with Eric.

"Lifestyle status."

"OK, at least now I know it's something personal. That's a start. But right now, I just don't have time to do this. It's been a rough day. I'm tired. And I'm about to become just as cranky as you are. So, how about I just get up and leave before one of us says something we can't take back? Maybe tomorrow night, when you've had a chance to lighten up, and I've had a chance to deal with some choices I'm making, we can take Matthew and go grab a pizza. Take this problem between us out of the workplace and see where we stand—*on everything*. Because I like you, or, I'm trying to, and I still want us to be friends again." More than she'd realized until just a little while ago. Despite his moods, Caleb was steady, and she needed that. And direction. And someone who didn't have to be *on* all the time, the way Eric had. All that was Caleb.

"Do you even remember when we used to be friends, Leanne?" he asked, finally looking at her, even though his eyes were as unrelenting as they had been ever since she'd sat down with him.

"Yes," she said tentatively, wondering where this was leading. "Why?" She had strong memories of their early childhood, but vague memories from when they were older. For some reason, Caleb didn't register with her the way she thought he should have during that time, and she didn't want to admit that to him. Didn't want him to know that, for her, part of their history had been so forgettable. Because that would only make him angrier, and she didn't think she could handle any more. Not now. Maybe not ever, if this was the real Caleb Carsten coming at her.

"I was just curious. That's all."

That's all? He was curious? Leanne let out a heavy sigh. It shouldn't take this much effort to be somebody's friend, but right now he was wearing her down. Making her wonder if he, or their friendship, was worth the effort she was trying to put into it. "Look, do you want to have pizza tomorrow, or not?" she finally asked, not even caring that she sounded irritated.

"Maybe." Said with no emotion, no real interest, like he was listening to a telephone solicitor just to be polite but not really hearing a word being said. "We do pizza night once a week. So maybe we'll run into you at Marco's. Or not."

"Fine," she said, spinning around and heading for the door. She'd had her full load of frustration for the day and she was done. "I hope you and Matthew have a good time," she said on her retreat. This was insanity. Pure insanity.

"We'll be there at six thirty," he finally called after her. No inflection in his voice whatsoever. And that's all he said.

Talk about a churlish invitation. If that was an invitation, it was so ungracious it sent shivers up her arms. Left her wondering why she'd ever suggested it in the first place. She turned back to face him. "Tell me now, Caleb. What did I do that's making you so angry with me? I'd like to get it resolved before Matthew gets dragged into it."

"I'm not dragging my son into anything between us, Leanne," he said.

"So, there *is* something between us?" Now she was more curious than ever. "What, Caleb?"

Rather than answering right away, though, he shut his eyes for a moment and shook his head. Then slowly he opened his eyes again and stared across the table at her. "I overheard some of your phone conversation earlier."

"Which one?"

"The one where you dumped your boyfriend."

"You mean the one where I was responding to the fact that he's cheating on me? *That* phone conversation? So, what's that got to do with you? Or us?"

Caleb's face went red, and he brushed an anxious hand through his hair. "He was cheating on you?"

"Apparently, since I wasn't the object of the last text he sent me. But what I don't understand, Caleb, is your attitude. What would my breakup with Eric have to do with you?"

"It just sounded like a conversation I'd heard before. You called me pathetic once, you know? Told me you never wanted to see me again."

"When?" She didn't remember that, but if she'd said that to him, why had he hung on to it for so long? It didn't make sense, especially since they'd only been kids back then, and kids did stupid things.

"One night, up at Eagle Pointe."

Where was this going? It was making her head spin, and she simply wasn't in the mood to cope. Not with anything or anyone. Whatever the misunderstanding had been, she'd straighten it out later. Or never, depending on Caleb. Right now, though, all she wanted to do was go home, shut the bedroom door behind her, pull the covers up over her head and pray for sleep. Which, she was sure, wouldn't show up. "Look, if we had a fight up at Eagle Pointe once, I don't remember it. Sorry. But right now..." She took in a deep breath and walked away. Didn't look back, even though she was sure he was staring at her. How did she know? The goose bumps. Always the goose bumps with Caleb. Then, and now.

* * *

Well, he'd opened his mouth and put his foot right in, and he felt bad. She'd been cheated on, and he'd just compounded the problem. It seemed he owed her another apology. But what he didn't understand was why she was avoiding what had happened that night. Why she claimed she didn't remember it. She did. Everybody in Marrell did.

Since she'd called to tell him she would be joining them for pizza after all, he would apologize. But would she apologize to him? For anything?

"One hour, Dad," Matthew yelled from the hallway. "One hour for the pizza, then I need to come home and practice."

"Leanne might be a slow eater," Caleb said on his way to the closet to pull out a shirt to go with his well-worn jeans. Frankly, it surprised him she'd agreed to meet them there. His invitation hadn't been friendly. Hadn't really been an invitation. And his attitude—well, that was something he needed to work on. At least the quick-trigger part of it. She brought out the bad in him, though, and while part of him thought she deserved it, a growing part disagreed with that. A growing part of him wished they could start all over. "It may take her longer than an hour to eat her pizza."

"We'll just have to tell her to hurry."

Perfect logic in such a young mind. Had his own mind ever been that logical? Because lately it was anything but. "That's not the polite thing to do. If someone eats slowly, we have to wait for them."

"Why?"

He smiled at his son, who was standing in the hall, looking deadly serious. "Would you like it if you went out to eat with someone who was much faster than you, and who left the table before you were only halfway through your meal?"

"It might make me eat faster."

"I know, so you could go home and practice. Look, buddy. Your audition's still three days away, and you're going to do fine. So right now, let's just concentrate on a pizza with pepperoni, mushrooms and extra cheese." He winked at

Matthew. "And anchovies. Great big ones. With eyes in them that are looking at you."

Matthew scrunched his face. "I hate anchovies! And anchovies don't have eyes."

"Then what do they see with?" Caleb asked him, trying to keep a straight face. It wasn't too often that Matthew got stumped on the little things, and he was enjoying this. Enjoying watching his son struggle through the reasoning process to find his answer.

Finally, when Matthew realized he didn't even know what an anchovy was, he asked, "Dad, what's an anchovy?"

"It's a tiny fish—" Caleb gestured to indicate about four inches in length "—with a big mouth—" he gestured to his own mouth, only larger "—and huge black eyes." He indicated saucer-sized eyes, and ran after Matthew, still gesturing those saucer-sizers, grabbed him up and tickled him.

"No," Matthew half squealed, half laughed.

"Yes," Caleb said, dropping Matthew down on the bed, then pouncing on top of him, still tickling him. It was so nice when Matthew let himself be a little boy. These moments were rare, and Caleb enjoyed every one of them.

"I can get away," Matthew warned, trying to squirm his way out from under his dad. He did so, for about a second, then Caleb caught hold of him, and pulled him right back, only this time not to tickle him but to hug him. Normally Matthew resisted displays of affection, and Caleb was surprised that he allowed the hug for a good ten seconds before he tugged out of it and ran away, calling after him, "No anchovies!"

He loved that kid. Until Matthew, he hadn't had a clue what love was about. He'd known the derivatives of it—lust, liking, affection, fondness. But Matthew had taught him love, and new ways to do it every single day. To look at him was to love him, and if that's all Caleb could do for the rest of his life—just look at Matthew—he'd be the happiest man in the world. Actually, he *was* the happiest man in the world. And the luckiest.

The pizza was getting cold, but Matthew hadn't found just the right angle from which to snap its picture, so Leanne and Caleb sat at the table and watched the boy pose the pizza every which way imaginable. Leanne was glad the three of them were spending this time together, glad Caleb was over his moodiness. Glad she'd changed her mind ten different times and finally decided to join them and, hopefully, straighten things out.

Because when Caleb wasn't being moody, well…at this point in her life, there really wasn't anybody else she enjoyed being around the way she did Caleb. Sad to say, but she'd been isolating herself for so long. All work, then time for Eric when she'd been able to. But there was nothing at all isolating about being with Caleb. He simply laid it out there, take it or leave it. Amazing how taking it had become something she almost wanted to do. Without the attitude switches midstream, of course.

"Dad and Dora are taking off for a long weekend," she said, as Matthew climbed up on a chair and knelt over the pizza to get a straight-down shot of it. "They're going to Helena, for what Dora's calling a civilized weekend. Dining, dancing, shopping at someplace other than a trading post. I'm glad they finally recognized how much they belong together."

"After how many years?" Caleb asked.

Leanne blew out a long, contemplative breath and shook her head. "Probably going on to thirty."

"That's a long time to wait to find your true love."

"Especially when she's been right there all this time." Leanne relaxed back into her chair and smiled. "Better late than never, I suppose."

"Sometimes never is better than anything else," Caleb quipped.

"You're referring to your marriage?" she asked him.

"If that's what you want to call it. She was *not* what I would have chosen if I'd been in the mood to look for a wife. Which I wasn't."

"Yet you married her." She thought back to all the men she'd dated over the years, and none of them had ever fit. Not truly. Not even Eric, which was why she wasn't as torn up about his other girlfriend as she might have been, or even should have been. And it wasn't that she didn't want to be married, because she did. But all the men queued up in her past had been too focused on other things—career, money, themselves. *Other women.* She wasn't sure why that was the type she'd always reeled in, but it was, and she was tired of the grind. So much so she was beginning to give up on the notion that it still might be out there for her. "You took the plunge, signed the papers, did whatever married couples do."

"Because..." He didn't say the words, but nodded at Matthew. "I wanted to do the right thing by her. So, we had a baby right off. And I don't regret anything about that. But our little sham of a marriage was only a bump in the road, and I think we both knew that at the start of it. We weren't suited. Didn't communicate or interact much. It was like we lived our separate lives, and the only thing that ever brought us together was..." He nodded at Matthew again. "And even then, that wasn't too often. I think I always looked at our divorce as the formality of ending something that had never really started in the first place."

"But you got Matthew." She, too, looked over

at the boy, who'd taken about twenty shots of the pizza, and was now sitting, waiting to eat a piece of it.

"And he was worth every second of those inconveniences of being married." Caleb put a slice of pizza on Matthew's plate, then one on Leanne's, and took one for himself.

"Would you do it again?"

"Maybe. Don't know for sure. I like the idea of a perfect little family, but disrupting what I already have scares the hell out of me. And I have to think about what's best for Matthew. So, maybe, one day I'll think about getting married again. *If* any woman would have me at that point."

Leanne laughed. "Oh, I think you'll be haveable. If you want to be. Question is, do you want to be?"

"Honestly, I don't know what I want to be. At least, not in my future. As far as my present…" He pointed at Matthew, who was ear-to-ear pizza sauce. "Seems about perfect to me."

"Well, for what it's worth, *perfect* shows on him. You're a great dad." Because she'd been raised without a mother, she knew how empty it had felt. But Matthew wasn't empty, the way she'd been. His life was full and Caleb worked hard to make it that way. He was the kind of dad every child deserved. "So, is the pizza good?" she asked Matthew.

He nodded. "But it's not healthy." He looked up at Caleb and smiled. "Right, Dad?"

"Right, buddy," Caleb said, giving Matthew the thumbs-up. "A lot of calories, a lot of fat."

"But it's good," Leanne added, biting her lip to keep from laughing at Matthew's seriousness. When she'd been his age, she'd been all into junk candy, soda and anything else that hadn't been good for her. Plus, she'd had a dad who'd traded time and attention for junk food gratification, so for her it had worked out.

"In moderation," Matthew said, reaching for his second slice.

"Do you even know what moderation means?" Caleb asked him. "Or is that just a word you've read?"

Matthew shrugged.

"Moderation means staying within reasonable

limits. Not having or doing too much. Do you understand that?"

Matthew looked up, grinned, and shook his head. "It means having two pieces of pizza instead of three."

"That's my boy," Caleb said, the look of pride on his face unmistakable.

This was nice, Leanne decided as she debated taking a second slice of pizza or heeding Matthew's warning that it wasn't good for her. The warnings of a five-year-old. She chuckled. Caleb was handling that situation just right.

CHAPTER FIVE

"ARE YOU SURE you want me here?" Leanne asked.

"He wants you to take pictures." Caleb handed her Matthew's camera, then led her through the door into the waiting area of Hans Schilling's school. "I told him I would, but he didn't trust me to do a good enough job." He was dressed in a business suit today, charcoal gray with a light blue dress shirt, clean shaven, no boots. Handsome as the devil and nervous as hell.

"You know he's going to do just fine," she said, patting Caleb on the hand.

"This is worse than when I took my medical boards, and I was pretty nervous about that."

"Was Matthew nervous this morning?" she asked him.

"I don't think the kid gets nervous about anything. He got up, ate his usual cereal, showered, brushed his teeth, got dressed, gathered up his music and walked out to the truck like it was any other day. But me—I couldn't eat, I used hand sanitizer rather than shampoo, tried on three suits and four shirts, put on socks that didn't match, and took a couple of antacid pills to settle my stomach. Then couldn't find the keys to my truck, which were in the bowl on the kitchen table—same place I always put them."

"It's an important day for you," she said.

Caleb shook his head. "Not for me. For Matthew. He needs this."

"And he'll get it. I met Schilling briefly the other day. He came to have a routine physical from Dad, and we chatted in passing. He seems to have great insight into life in general. I'm sure he'll see the talent and the potential Matthew has, and accept him."

"Wish I was that confident," Caleb grumbled. The waiting area in the recital hall resembled a lodge, much like everything in Marrell did. Lots of wood, wide-open spaces and rustic decor. Not the kind of place he would have expected from a world-renowned pianist but, then, he'd never known a world-renowned pianist before, so he really didn't know what to expect. "But Matthew's only been in there five minutes, and I'm ready to fall apart."

"How long does the total audition take?"

"About two hours. He'll hear Matthew play first, then ask him questions. After which he'll give him an academic test to make sure he can be placed appropriately, if accepted."

"Then it sounds to me like Matthew's going to have a pretty easy time of it."

"Except that he's two years younger than the children Schilling normally accepts. His starting age is seven, and he's making a huge exception for Matthew, just auditioning him." Thanks, largely, to his grandmother's apple pies and Hans Schilling's voracious appetite for them.

"When he's accepted—and you notice I said when, not if—will he live here?"

"That's a requirement. Schilling likes to keep the kids close, so he can see to the proper discipline they need, both academically as well as musically."

"And Matthew's agreeable to that?"

"He's agreeable to anything that will allow him to practice on a concert grand piano. Which I don't happen to have." Having Matthew leave him, even if he'd only be a few miles away, was something Caleb wasn't sure how he was going to handle. Schilling allowed liberal visiting hours. Parents were welcome anytime except during practice hours, and they could come and go as often as they pleased. Schilling also allowed plenty of time for the children to go out with their parents for hours, even for a few days when the schedule permitted. So, it wasn't like he and Matthew were going to be separated forever. They weren't. He'd see him every day. But he'd only be tucking him into bed on the weekends, when Matthew came home to visit, and to Caleb, that already felt like hell. "It's a good program, and Matthew needs that kind of structure in his life, especially with his…"

"Gifts?" Leanne supplied.

"Right now, he's easy because he's only five. But I can see the time coming when I won't be able to give him everything he needs. Academically maybe. Emotionally definitely. But musically… For Matthew, it's all tied up in one tight little ball that I can't untie. That's where Schilling comes in. He works with the parents of children like Matthew. Teaches them how to take care of their children's special talents."

"So, when will Matthew be leaving?" she asked.

Caleb moaned. "Too soon. School's on hiatus for six weeks right now, but in another couple of weeks it'll resume, and I'm afraid my life is going to change in ways I don't even want to think about." He dreaded that day, didn't know how he was going to get through it. But this was about Matthew, not him. "And I'm not looking forward to it. But you do what you have to do to take care of your kid."

"Unlike my father, who did anything he could to occupy himself with work and not me… Anyway, can I get you some coffee, Caleb?" Leanne asked. "Or prescribe you a tranquilizer?"

"Was Henry really that bad?"

"Dad was never bad. He just never had time. I think he counted on my mother to raise me, and when she died, he didn't know what to do. So, he didn't do anything."

"I guess I never saw that." Probably because there had been too many other things to see, and deal with.

"When I was younger, I didn't either. But as I got older…" She shook her head. "Anyway, about that coffee…"

He could see by the melancholy look on her face that this wasn't a topic she wanted to talk about. So, he rooted around the rest of the questions he wanted to ask, like, *Would you have been less of a bully if your dad had paid more attention to you?* Or, *Was your bullying merely a way to get your dad's attention?* He played it safe. For now. "Just keep talking to me. That'll work."

Forcing herself to smile a smile that never quite made it all the way to genuine, she held up the camera. "How about I take a picture of you?" She clicked before he had time to protest. "And another, since Matthew likes multiples of the same thing."

"He likes to analyze them for subtle differences. He told me no two pictures are ever the same." Caleb walked over to the front window, the one with the expansive view of the meadow in the foreground and the river in the background. A movie crew was filming down at the river today—an adventure movie, he'd heard. Meaning Marrell was brimming with activity—something entirely new for him. Something to indicate his little town really *was* growing up. "I appreciate you taking time off work to come with us. I know Matthew wanted you here for himself, but I think I need you more than he does." Because, quite simply, he liked being around Leanne. It was conflicting, it was troubling, but none of that stopped him. Like it hadn't stopped him all those years ago. Except he was older now. Knew better. *He hoped.*

"That's what old friends are for," she said, backing away from the concert grand in the lodge's lobby, then taking a picture of it. "Will they let us in to see Matthew during any part of the interview? Because I'd like to get some pictures."

"Right now, they're going over some of the preliminaries with him, but when he plays, we can watch him from an observation booth."

"Dr. Carsten?"

Caleb spun around to face the tall, austere blonde woman who was standing in the doorway through which Matthew had disappeared moments earlier. "Yes?" he asked, tentatively, as his momentary lapse of nerves was exiting and a new round tromping in.

"You and your guest are welcome to join us in the studio. Matthew is becoming acquainted with the piano, and Maestro Schilling will be joining him momentarily. So, if you'd like to follow me, I'll be glad to explain the next part of the process to you, and allow you a minute or two with Matthew before he proceeds into the audition portion of this interview."

"And take pictures?" Leanne asked.

"Of course." The woman turned and headed into the studio, leaving Caleb and Leanne to follow.

"He looks so small at that piano," Leanne said, in almost a whisper, as they entered the studio. "And serious." Aiming the camera, she took a couple of pictures from the back of the room, then simply stood back and watched him for a minute. He was so like Caleb was, and it stirred an unexpected emotion in her. Pride. Even though Matthew wasn't hers, she had so much pride in him her heart was swelling with it.

"You can go talk to him," the blonde woman said, interrupting Leanna's thoughts. "He doesn't seem nervous, but most children like to have a little reassurance from their parents before this part of the interview commences."

"Thank you," Leanne said, giving Caleb a nudge forward. "You go down there. I'll stay here and get a picture of it."

"If my legs will carry me that far," he said, as nervous sweat started to break out on his forehead.

"You're not going to hyperventilate, are you?" she whispered to him.

"If I do, it's a good thing I brought a doctor along with me, isn't it?"

Leanne laughed. "Go talk to him, Caleb. He may appear unfazed, but he's only five and he needs your support." Before she left the observation area, she stretched up on tiptoe and brushed his lips lightly with a kiss. A kiss that, oddly, tingled on her lips. And one that she repeated, for a second or two longer than the first.

He looked stunned at first. Looked as taken aback as she felt. But his expression gave way quickly to a smile. "I'm sorry, I didn't..." she began, but stopped. Now wasn't the time to try explaining this, or even wonder why she'd done it, because she didn't know. Caleb had looked vulnerable and she supposed she had been responding to that. But she wasn't sure. "For luck," she finally conceded, then walked away before he had the chance to see the red flush creeping its way up her neck.

"Thank you," he called after her, as she headed up to the observation booth while he headed down to the stage.

She ignored that, however. Just kept on walking until she was at the top of the bowl-shaped performance area, and safely tucked away in the observation booth. Leaning against the wall. Eyes shut. Breathing hard from embarrassment or distress or whatever else was bothering her about giving him a stupid little kiss.

Caleb spent the next two minutes talking to Matthew, who didn't seem daunted by anything going on, even though he himself was daunted by that kiss. It was probably just as Leanne had said...for luck. But what if it wasn't? And why was it more on his mind right now than Matthew's audition? *Because she'd never kissed him before, that's why.* Not even in those few years when they'd been childhood friends. And there'd been so many times when he'd wanted that kiss and had known he'd never get it.

Well, he'd got it now, and it was distracting him at a time when everything he wanted for his son was walking through the door and taking a seat, getting ready to pass judgment. "Look, Matthew," Caleb whispered in the boy's ear, shaking himself back into the moment, "You know you can do this. Leanne and I will be up there..." He pointed to the glassed off section at the top of the room. "So, if anything..." He stopped, regrouped, then took a deep breath. "I love you," he said. "And I'm proud of you." Then retreated to the observation room to have a silent breakdown.

On his way up the stairs, Caleb nodded at Schilling, finally allowing himself a good look at the man. Aged well into his seventies, with long gray-white hair and impeccable navy blue suit, he sported an ascot. Red paisley print. Very proper old-world man, Caleb decided, then smiled and relaxed when Matthew giggled at something Schilling whispered to him.

"This is going to work," he said, scooting back to the edge of his chair in the observation room, his relaxation short-lived as he watched Matthew squirm his way into position on the piano bench.

"Matthew looks like you did when you were that age," Leanne said.

"Does he?"

"You were always so serious, like you had an agenda with the world. Even when we played, you were always focused on something else. Something I couldn't see, or didn't understand. Like Matthew is always so focused."

"And ostracized for it," he said flatly.

"You weren't," she said. "Not that I remember. I think people were a little afraid of you because you were so smart, but I liked you. Liked listening to you, even though I didn't understand half of what you were telling me."

And she'd liked ridiculing him when they got older.

How could her memories be so different from his?

This was turning into a trust issue. He wanted to, thought he did, but there was this unsettled little part of him that still warned him to be wary. "Well, Matthew's a whole lot smarter than I was, and he's certainly more talented. I think when I was five my only talent was making mud pies."

"My dad said you used to drag home stray animals, that you had your own little zoo going. And you'd care for those animals. Pretend to be their doctor. He said you were actually pretty talented at discovering some simple illnesses, even at that age."

So, she was talking to her dad about him? Yet forgetting, or pretending to forget, how things had really been? Nope, none of this was making sense to him and he wondered if Leanne was still living in a fairy-princess world where she could have things her way simply because she wanted them to be? "Haven't had a pet since I left Marrell. If we stay here, I might get Matthew a puppy. He keeps telling me he wants one, and I think it will be good for him."

"I've never had a pet. My dad didn't have time to take care of one, and I wasn't responsible enough." She chuckled. "In fact, Dad told me I wasn't responsible about a lot of things when I was young. He said it used to worry him."

And she was sitting next to the living proof of her irresponsibility. Not remembering, or not caring enough to remember. Or maybe it had been so common with her—a second nature that he always excused because of his other feelings— that it just floated right on past her? "I remember some of that," he said, as the lights dimmed in the studio, and the observation room speakers were turned on so they could hear what was going on.

Leanne leaned over and took hold of his hand. And he didn't resist her. Didn't shove her away.

In fact, he was glad of her comfort. Wasn't sure he liked being glad of it, but he was, nonetheless.

"Mr. Carsten," Hans Schilling said, addressing Matthew. "I see, by your application, I'm going to hear to hear Chopin's Fantaisie-Impromptu, Opus 66. But, Matthew, because I know your hands are still too small to accomplish this piece as it should be played, I'd like you to commence at the key change, beginning with the *moderato cantabile*, going through the next key change so I can assess how you handle the faster passages, ending just after the *sempre crescendo* just before you get to the *forte* chord. Do you understand where that is in the score?"

"Yes, sir," Matthew said, his voice confident and strong.

"Then, please, begin anytime you're ready."

In the observation booth, Caleb sucked in a deep breath and held it, and didn't let it go until Matthew played his first note, which seemed an eternity. In slow motion. Then it all went by in a blur. Caleb recognized the music, but he was more intent on watching Schilling for a reaction. So, he focused on the maestro, and the music flowed on, perfectly as far as he could tell. And Leanne's hold on his hand turned into a harder squeeze, getting harder and harder as the audition progressed. Still, he kept his eyes on Schilling, who gave nothing away. Then suddenly the music stopped, Leanne's squeeze on his hand let up, Matthew stepped away from the piano bench and took a bow to the single applauding member of the audience. It was over. All those months of work and this was it. Caleb didn't know whether to stand up and cheer or melt into a nervous breakdown on the floor.

He wiped the sweat off his forehead with the back of his hand, slumped back in his seat, and finally allowed himself to breathe. Then looked over and smiled at Leanne, who was slumped back much the way he was.

"He's stunning," she whispered, wiping tears from her eyes. "I never expected... Caleb, I can't even tell you how wonderful he is."

Caleb nodded, fighting back his own tears. "He is," he whispered in return.

"Now, Mr. Carsten, referring to your repertoire list, I see that you have listed Mozart's Piano

Sonata No. 16 in C Major, K. 545. Do you have that committed to memory?"

"I commit everything to memory, sir," Matthew answered, not in the least shy.

"Please, then, start at the beginning and play until I tell you to stop."

"He hasn't practiced that one for the audition," Caleb said, sucking in another sharp breath and scooting back to the edge of his seat. "Why would Schilling do that to him?"

"He'll be fine," Leanne said, scooting to the edge of her own seat again and taking hold of Caleb's hand once more, like it was the natural thing to do between them now. "And maybe Schilling's doing that because he's so impressed he wants to see the full of extent of Matthew's talent."

"It's killing me. Just killing me. And look at my son. He's calm. How can he be that calm, Leanne?"

She laughed. "You're just being a typical parent, Caleb. But don't worry about Matthew. Do you see his face? *This* is the world where he belongs."

Caleb nodded, but nothing alleviated his nerves

as Matthew's melodious strains started to fill the studio. Surprisingly, Schilling listened to the entire first movement of the Mozart, rather than cutting it off. Then asked Matthew to perform another off his repertoire list, a Bach Two-part Invention. When the audition was over, Matthew hopped off the bench, took his bow, then asked Schilling for a drink of water.

"Through those doors at the rear," Schilling said, turning to the observation booth and gesturing for Caleb to join him. "The woman outside, Miss Dobson, will give you a drink. We also have lemonade and milk, if you'd prefer."

"Lemonade has sugar, which is not good for you, unless it's in *moderation*." He grinned at the use of his new word. "And I don't like milk so much."

"But our water here is very good. Healthy. Lots of beneficial minerals." Schilling laughed. "Make sure you tell Miss Dobson you want the healthy water."

Matthew nodded, then skipped out of the studio as Caleb and Leanne entered. "You know Dr. Sinclair," Caleb said, taking hold of Leanne's arm and leading her toward the front of the studio.

"Ah, yes. We met briefly just the other day. I'm assuming she'll be my new doctor, now that her father is retiring. And, I hope, the doctor who replaces her father as the school doctor."

Leanne shook her head. "That won't be me, but I think Dr. Carsten here can be persuaded."

"Very good," Schilling said, extending a hand to Caleb. "Now, about Matthew..." Schilling's warm smile grew wider. "The audition went well. Much better than I anticipated. And I love his intellect. He reminds me of myself when I was his age. Too intelligent, and very gifted, without the proper instruction on how to deal with it. My parents tried, but I was...different. And that can be quite a burden for someone so young, which is why I created the school: to start children like Matthew off in a direction that better suits their capabilities. And educate their parents on how to handle such a special child. So, if everything else in this interview goes as I anticipate it will, I think Matthew will be a nice addition to our family, even though he's a bit younger than I'm used to training."

Caleb was so relieved to hear the news he didn't know if he wanted to laugh or cry. "I haven't been able to find the best teachers for him. He can be...intimidating, and I think he scares a lot of people because he does get a kick out of trying to present himself as knowing more than they do."

Schilling laughed. "Little tykes like that, especially ones with an attitude, don't intimidate me, no matter how good they are at the piano, and no matter how intelligent they are. In fact, it's my goal to intimidate them a little. Keeps them humble."

"He'll have time here to be just a regular little boy, won't he?" Leanne asked.

"Mandatory. Children like Matthew can get so wrapped up in their pursuits they lose their childhood, so I strive to make everything here as normal as I can, to teach these kids they must live *in* the world, and not separate from it. Accordingly, we have television, movies, video games, outdoor activities. Horses. Like I said, I grew up like Matthew—sheltered as a prodigy and a genius, and it's not a life any child should have, which is why we work for as much normalcy as we can get. And now, if you'll excuse me, I'm going to prepare for the interview portion of this, and if you two would like, please have a look around the property. Everything is open for your inspection." Then he exited the studio through the side door, leaving Caleb and Leanne standing there, Caleb simply staring into space while Leanne snapped photos.

"I think he's in," Caleb finally said.

"Was there ever any doubt?"

"Honestly, I'm not sure." He took hold of her arm and led her to the back door. "Anyway, care to take a walk with me?"

"If we could go outside so I can take some pictures. I want to make sure he gets this full day journaled, and that includes the riding stable out back."

"You two seem to share the same photographic interest," Caleb commented.

"I'd forgotten how much I loved it. When I was a child, my dad would let me wander around by myself a lot of the time because he was too busy to go with me. And I'd always take my camera because, with it, it wasn't so lonely being by my-self. I always had it as a distraction to keep my mind off how I was really feeling. But then I grew up and…" She shrugged. "You know how it is. Other interests take over."

In Leanne's case, her other interests had turned quite social. She'd been the popular girl in school, the one every other girl wanted as a friend, and every boy wanted to date. She'd known it, and had taken full advantage of it. But today wasn't the day to dwell on all that. It was Matthew's day, and Matthew was his focus. "Outside sounds perfect. Especially the stables. Matthew's been telling me he wants to learn to ride."

Leanne pointed the camera at his face and snapped. "That one's going to be titled 'Dad with Concerned Look.'"

Smiling, she spun around and flounced to the front door while Caleb held back and watched her. Caution and all, she was certainly hard to resist. Always had been.

"He's sleeping," Caleb said, closing the bedroom door behind him. The three of them had spent the entire day together. First the audition. Then ice cream. After that, Matthew had insisted on taking photos of Stiller's Well, a sizable sinkhole, fenced off for safety's sake, about twenty miles outside town. The trip out there took nearly two hours, as Matthew was so keyed up he wanted to stop every hundred feet for a photo. And the trip back took nearly as long, as Leanne asked to stop at an old trading post, where she bought herself a brand-new camera, zoom lenses, filters, tripods and other accessories.

Overall, it had been a nice day, other than his case of audition jitters, and he was pleased that Leanne was forging quite a bond with his son. It worried him, though, because he didn't want Matthew getting too attached to someone who'd already made it perfectly clear she wasn't staying. He'd sailed through his mother's abandonment like a little trouper, but he'd been only two, and the full impact of it might not have sunk in. But getting attached to Leanne, like he clearly was, and her leaving him...

"I think the day just wore him out. Normally, he's not in bed for a couple more hours."

Leanne sat on Caleb's butter-soft leather couch, shut her eyes and leaned her head back. "He gets tired easily because he's only five, Caleb. Sometimes I think you forget that."

"I do, because he's so…old."

"He's also barely more than a baby."

Caleb crossed the room and sprawled out in the chair across from Leanne rather than plopping down next to her. "I appreciate you being there. It could have turned into a long, difficult day for me, just sitting around, biting my nails and waiting for Matthew to get through his interviews."

"Well, one of the perks of owning the hospital is that I can schedule myself in and out any way I need to so long as everything's covered."

"So, what are you going to do, Leanne? Have you given it any thought?"

She shook her head. "Nothing solid after I leave here. Since my plans with Eric fell through—"

"Hard and ugly," he interrupted. "I'm sorry about that. And I'm also sorry for the things I said to you that day. I was wrong, and you didn't deserve it."

"Apology accepted. And, overall, the breakup

could have been worse. I might have actually planned my life around him. Instead, I was still in the planning on planning my life around him stage. Really messed up, huh?"

"Well, then, I'm sorry your life is so messed up."

"Messed up *and* transitional." She grimaced. "Sounds pretty bad, doesn't it?"

"Well, for what it's worth, I know how you feel. Been there myself."

"So, you know the end of the story? Please tell me you do." She smiled at him. "Please tell me how it turns out."

Caleb chuckled. "Wish I could. But I haven't reached the end yet, and I don't have a clue what it's going to be. As for you, I suppose your ending can actually turn into a beginning."

"That sounds interesting, especially since I'm wondering if I can even go back and work in the same hospital with him. And since I know he's not going anywhere…guess that leaves me in a *me or him* kind of a situation, doesn't it?"

"I'm curious. What do you say in matters like this? Sorry for your loss?"

"More like, good riddance." Leanne straightened up on the sofa. "So, as far as what I'll be doing next, I don't know. Maybe take some more time off and hang around here a while longer. Or look for another position in Seattle, because I really do love it there. He took a lot from me, Caleb. My dignity. My reputation. Probably my job. And I feel so...unsure."

"Unsure isn't easy," he said, commiserating with her yet, at the same time, thinking back on all the times she'd made *him* feel unsure. Wishing those thoughts would just go away because the here-and-now Leanne was the one he'd always wanted her to be. The memories wouldn't disappear, though. No matter how hard he tried to force them away, they were still hanging in as a warning. A guard against letting down *his* guard. "I suppose you either ignore it, or embrace it. If you ignore it, you pretend none of it matters, or didn't happen." Like how she was ignoring the uncertainties she'd heaped on him. "If you embrace it, you let it teach you a lesson." How not to trust so easily. How not to be so gullible the way he'd been. And, to an extent, was now.

"Well, even though I don't know where I'm going, I do know where I'm not staying. So, after this audition, I'm expecting your answer. And Eric…well, that's water under the bridge. I'm moving on. Not sure which direction, but that really doesn't bother me so much because I've always liked new directions. Old ones get…boring."

She was so matter-of-fact about it. Out with the old, in with the new. For a moment, he thought he'd seen a true change in her. But now he wondered. *Again*. Back and forth. Seeing the changes, then unseeing them because she was taking this the way she took everything else—brushing it aside for something else.

Caleb frowned to cover his disappointment. This *was* the old Leanne sitting here in front of him now. Just a more mature version than the one he'd known before. As much as he didn't want her to be, the signs were all there. "Want something to eat? Or drink?" he asked, trying to put it out of his mind the way she did.

"That hamburger we had after the interview was plenty for me, but I wouldn't mind something to drink."

"Wine? Coffee? Water?" Asked hospitably, even though he was ready for her to go. She weighed him down emotionally. Raised his hopes, let them down. And right now, he was too tired to fend for himself. Too tired to cope.

"Wine would be good," she said.

"Red or white?" he asked, not wholeheartedly into the evening with her anymore.

"Surprise me with the wine." Leanne watched Caleb get up and walk into the kitchen. Admired the look of him. Strong. Nicely muscled. He looked like her fantasy version of a cowboy, and she liked that. She liked Caleb, hot *or* cold. Was it because she had expectations of him that reached as far back as their childhoods? Or new expectations that had nothing to do with who they'd been then? Absolutely, she was attracted. Physically, emotionally, intellectually. Even when he turned cold on her, like he was doing now. It didn't go away. In fact, it made her want to push on through and get to the other side. Because there was another side. With Caleb, there always had been. "Why weren't we better friends back in school?" she called out to him, out of the blue.

Caleb dropped the wineglass he was holding into the sink, where it shattered into hundreds of clear shards. He looked down at the mess, blew out a frustrated breath, then reached for another wineglass. "I wasn't in your league," he called back, his voice as rigid as a taut trip wire.

Leanne blinked hard. "I'm not aware that I had a league." She'd been popular, sure. Her dad had been the wealthiest man in town, which wasn't saying a whole lot since the town was so small. And maybe she had let that go to her head a little. But being in any particular league? No, she didn't understand that at all.

"You *were* the league," he said, reappearing in the living room, holding two glasses of red wine.

She studied him for a moment. Yes, he was in his *mood* again, and she'd caused it, but she didn't know how. "Which means?"

He crossed the room, handed her the stemmed glass, then returned to his chair across from her.

Sitting rigidly. Ramrod straight. Unyielding. "Which means you had your group of friends, and you weren't really interested in letting anybody else into it."

"Aren't all teenagers that way, though?" she asked him, still perplexed by the direction of this conversation. Not only was his body language angry now, so were his words. And his eyes... narrowed in such coldness it almost scared her.

"I wasn't. But, then, I was always the outsider, looking in." He took a sip of wine. "Had a good, long look from that vantage point."

"Caleb, I know we grew apart, but we were kids. That happens." Honestly, those days were so vague, she really didn't dredge them up too often. Probably because she sorted her life into two categories: Marrell, and post-Marrell. Nothing about Marrell had ever registered very much with her, as she'd spent her entire time here looking for ways to get out. And anything that had had even the slightest potential of stopping her had gotten discarded.

Had she, somehow, perceived Caleb as having the potential to stop her? Was that why they'd grown apart? She didn't know. Couldn't dredge up a memory. Got all sweaty and nervous when she tried.

"Yep, happens," he agreed, took another sip of wine.

"So maybe what you were interpreting as out of your league was more like two kids growing up and growing apart?" She knew that wasn't the answer. Could tell from his body language. And it was frustrating because she knew she was missing something she should know. Something he should be telling her, but wasn't.

"What I was interpreting was that you were high society and I was the boy who swept up the clinic floors. The one who got hauled off to the town lockup more times than I can count, who eventually ended up in the county jail, then a state juvenile detention center. You know, the boy who never could get *the* girl."

Had she been *the* girl for him? She didn't remember it that way. In fact, she only remembered being crushed when he'd turned away from her. "But a lot of girls go after the bad boys."

"Except I wasn't a bad boy, Leanne. I was a

misguided boy, and a very confused one, and that's a big difference. Bad boys want to be bad to make an impression. Misguided boys just want to fit in."

"So, you're describing yourself as confused back then?"

He took another sip of wine. "I'm describing myself as a boy who got warned, over and over, but stepped into it, anyway."

"What, Caleb? What did you step into?" She wanted to know. No more hints and vague accusations. "If there's something specific I'm missing…or missed back then, tell me. I have a right to know."

"You missed *me*, Leanne. I was head over heels crazy about you, and you missed it. Or took advantage of it. I'm not sure which. But, however it was, I was too dumb to know what I was doing at the time, although I learned my lesson eventually, and it's the lesson I'm going to teach Matthew. Because he's different, the way I was, and I don't ever want him to be the outsider who has to content himself with just looking in."

He stopped, shook his head, then forced a tight

smile. One that made her uncomfortable. So, she forged ahead. "I guess I never knew it was that bad for you, and I'm sorry for that. Of course, all I was doing was trying to find a way out, so there may have been a lot of things I didn't notice."

"Yet, here you are, back again."

"Same could be said of you, Caleb. You're back, too," she said, the annoyance in her voice obvious. He was accusing her of things she didn't know, didn't understand, and she had no way to fight back or defend herself. So, she wasn't going to engage. What was the point, when she'd only be fighting a demon she couldn't even see? Instead, she forced herself to relax. Take a deep breath. Refocus. "And that seems to be working out."

"Because I'm back for Matthew. *Not* for me. I didn't have a choice because I wanted to be a better dad to him."

She took a sip of her own wine, then shook her head.

"Like I had to come back to help my dad. I

never realized how alike we are. Both of us taking care of the greater obligations in our lives."

"And there you are, changing the subject, like what was between us never existed."

"There *wasn't* anything between us, Caleb." The annoyance was bubbling up. Again. "You might have been crazy about me, but I wasn't about to let anything or anybody stand in my way, and I took care not to get involved. So much so, I didn't even know you wanted to become a doctor."

"I think *everybody* in Marrell who ever cared about me knew I wanted to be a doctor."

And she hadn't. Two kids from the same small town, former best friends with the same goal, and she'd had no idea. But had Caleb, back then, been much like he was now—always keeping to himself, always trying to push people away? Was that why they hadn't struck up the friendship she'd believed they could have had, and maybe even should have had? What had she missed out on? Suddenly, Leanne was overwhelmed by the feeling that by excluding Caleb, as he said she'd done, she'd missed out on so much. "If I was too focused on myself to pay attention to you, I really am sorry. But I was struggling, Caleb."

"We were *all* struggling, Leanne. You, me... God only knows who else. Only no one else took it out on people the way you did."

There it was again. The hint of an accusation. Why was he doing this to her? "What did I do to you, Caleb?" It must have been something so significant to Caleb he'd never let it go, even after all these years. For her, she didn't even remember it. How could that be? She didn't want to deal with it now. Maybe later, but not now, not when she was so frustrated. So, maybe running away wasn't such a bad thing after all, because that's what she wanted to do right now. Run away from something she didn't understand, or couldn't see from his perspective.

"Look, I don't want to do this now. OK? I just want to go home." She gulped down the last of her wine and stood. "Tell Matthew I enjoyed the day, and thank him for asking me along." It had been Matthew's idea. Not Caleb's. Which was a little disappointing. "Also, tell him that if you're not busy Sunday afternoon, I have an awesome new photo editing program, and he's welcome to come over and use it." She looked up at Caleb, and wished…well, she didn't know what she wished. But it wasn't this distance between them. "You're welcome to come along, too. I might even be persuaded to cook."

As she brushed by Caleb on her way to the front door she stopped, looked up, and for some unknown reason stood on tiptoe and brushed a gentle kiss to his lips. Twice in one day. It stunned her that she'd done that the first time, and stunned her yet again that she'd gone in for a second one. Especially since the evening had turned so tense. But it felt right. Even though he was totally not sending out signals of any kind, it still felt right to her. Almost natural, and she didn't regret it, because sometimes being impulsive led to things a person could never anticipate. With Caleb, she wasn't sure what that could be. But in spite of herself and, more to the point, in spite of him, she liked him. *And now he knew it.* "It really was a lovely day, Caleb. Thank you for including me. And for what it's worth—whatever it is we've got rocking back and forth between us, I want to be your friend. We've just got to figure out how, I think."

"Sunday," he said, his voice unusually calm. Almost subdued. Then suddenly he pulled her into him roughly and kissed her back, but not in the light way she'd kissed him. More like the way a hungry man kissed a woman he wanted. Craved. Desired.

And as his mouth opened to her, and she felt his tongue delve inside hers, she melted into him, into a kiss she'd never had before. Never come close to having. Never wanted to end. For that one moment, everything seemed simple. He was a man, she was a woman, both finally on the same journey. Yet when she dared brave a look up at him, she saw that he was looking her, his expression intense, almost threatening.

Was he still angry? Was it because of the way he responded to her now? She could definitely feel his hard response pressing at her. She wondered, but before she could ponder it further, he yanked her even harder to him and pressed her mouth even more, probed even deeper. Moaned.

She responded immediately, surprising herself.

Wanting more of him. Snaking her hands around his neck to hold him there. His mouth was so warm, the press of his lips insistent. And she was so eager for anything, everything, preparing herself for it, wanting it so badly. But as the realization of what she was doing was sweeping over her, his kiss lightened, turned into a whisper, then disappeared. Then he stepped back. Cleared his throat, ran his hand through his hair. And looked…stunned. Not angry. Just stunned.

"Well, that was—" he started.

"Unexpected," she finished, wishing she had something to fan herself with.

"I was going to say nice. But unexpected works." He took another step backward, then smiled awkwardly. "Anyway…"

"Yes, anyway…" Talk about the need to diffuse an uncomfortable moment. But for the life of her, she couldn't think of a graceful way out of it. So, she simply took a few steps backward herself, turned to the door and opened it. Then left. Quickly. Confused. No words. Practically running down his front steps. Not stopping. Not even looking back. But she did hear the click of the door shutting behind her and wondered, for an instant, if he was watching her out the side-light. Hoped he was. Hoped he took that kiss to bed with him and it kept him awake for a while, because it would surely keep her awake.

Yep, she liked Caleb despite himself. Couldn't explain why, didn't really want to. And if she decided to stay in Marrell for a while longer, she wondered how far she would let that fondness for him go. Wondered how far *he* would let it go before he stopped it. Because she had an idea that he didn't let anything personal in his life go on for too long before he put an end to it. Pity, as she had a hunch that, deep down, he had a lot to offer. Of course, she wasn't going to stay around long enough, or get herself that entangled, to find out what.

CHAPTER SIX

IT WAS SEVEN in the morning now, and he was exhausted: exhausted from too much thinking, from pacing back and forth, from wondering and worrying. All night long. Minute after minute, hour after hour. Unrelenting confusion. Even Matthew had noticed, and that wasn't good because this was something he didn't need his son involved in. Five, albeit a genius five, was too young to be carrying around adult woes. Yet as he dropped Matthew off at his parents' house this morning, his little boy seemed to be weighed down by the same stresses that were weighing on him. Shuffling little gait, slumped shoulders, heavy sighs...

Caleb shut his eyes and sighed heavily himself. Why was he falling for Leanne? Again? He'd vowed not to. Even last night, after that kiss, he'd promised himself he wouldn't go near that again. Yet if she walked in here right now, stopped at the nursing desk and kissed him the way she had, he wasn't sure he could, or would, resist it. And that was why he was starting his day on exactly zero hours of sleep. Too tired to move. Or think. But not too tired to recognize his confusion, because it was there, in spades, threatening to bring him to his knees.

"So, what's first up this morning?" he asked Helen McBriarty, trying to infuse some life into his voice.

She was standing in the hallway outside his office door, waiting for him as he walked down the hall. She was also the mother of Scott McBriarty, someone who'd gotten into a lot of childhood trouble with him. Smoking, drinking, minor vandalism. To this day, Helen didn't like him and, judging from the scowl on her face this morning, she particularly didn't like the fact that he was ten minutes late. Or that he was working at Sinclair. Or that he'd even returned to Marrell. And with the way he was feeling right now, if she'd pointed to the door and told him to get out, the way she'd done so often when he'd turned up at her house for Scott, he might just take her up on it.

But no such luck. She shoved an old-fashioned clipboard at his chest and barked, "Rounds. You have five patients admitted with general complaints. Same five you saw yesterday. Review committee meeting at eleven. Clinic starting at one. So far, you have nine appointments scheduled, with two tentatives who might show up as walk-ins. Oh, and because you were late this morning, I'm assuming you'll extend your hours at the end of the day to make up for it." She folded her arms across her ample bosom and tapped her foot impatiently. "We all go by the same rules around here, *Doctor*. No one person is better than another."

If anyone ever needed to be put in their place, Helen was the one to do it. But that wasn't a bad thing right now, because it was her testy demeanor that snapped him back to the present. "Actually, I'm scheduled until six, so that should cover any of my punctuality transgressions," he said, relieved to be back on track.

"Thanks, Helen," he said, then watched her

scowl deepen. She really did hate him. Had for a very long time. In fact, after the third time he and Scott had been hauled off to the town sheriff's office for being public nuisances, Helen had forbidden her son from having contact with Caleb again, which had made that forbidden friendship even more exciting. Did she know how often, after that, Scott had sneaked out his bedroom window to meet him? Judging from the look on her face, she probably did.

"*Mrs. McBriarty*, Doctor. I prefer to keep it professional."

"I'll remember that," Caleb said, as he walked away from her and headed to the wing where most of his patients were admitted. Marrell had changed in a lot of ways, but Helen McBriarty wasn't one of them. Somehow, that seemed fitting.

"I checked on Ella Jameson for you," Leanne said, greeting Caleb on his way into the wing as she was on her way out. "She was complaining of stomach pains, and because I was already on duty… Hope you don't mind."

Seeing her didn't cause the emotional flutter

he'd expected. But it wasn't an easy thing either. So, he kept his distance, stayed on the other side of the hall, like that little barrier would separate more than his body from hers. *And, damn, he wanted her body closer. Like last night.*

Caleb cleared his throat, then answered. "No, that's fine. Since I was late...ten minutes."

Leanne laughed. "Oh, Helen. She was on the warpath this morning, wasn't she?"

It was as if last night with her hadn't happened. Whatever happened happened. Then nothing. Like all those things she'd done when they'd been kids. The way she'd treated him, bullied him, made him the target of her agenda, whatever that had been, then...nothing. He didn't get how someone could just do something, then walk away from it so easily. Maybe even forget it. But that was Leanne, through and through, and it concerned him that he couldn't get past her blatant omissions. They bothered him, didn't faze her. "Well, from everything I hear, she's a great nurse. So, I guess she's entitled to go on the warpath every now and then."

"Or every time she sees you. You do know you rub her up the wrong way, don't you?"

"She made that painfully clear to me when I was fourteen years old, the same way she did five minutes ago."

Leanne fidgeted with the button on her white jacket for a moment, then frowned. "She holds you personally responsible for the way Scott turned out."

He noticed her nervousness and wondered if she was finally having a reaction to their kiss. "He does OK. Good job. Nice house. A couple of divorces. Except the divorces, what's so bad about that?"

"You got him arrested a couple of times."

"He got himself arrested. It just coincided with times when I was busy getting myself arrested."

"But you corrupted him, according to Helen. He was a good boy until he met you."

Caleb laughed out loud. "That's probably true. He got sent away shortly after I did. Juvenile crimes too many to count, I was told. And Helen wasn't happy about that. So, tell me, if I take over managing the hospital, how am I supposed to manage her?"

Leanne stopped fidgeting with her button and shoved her hands into her coat pockets. "You don't. You let her do what she wants, and get by the best way you can." Scooting around Caleb, she took every precaution not to brush up against him. So much so, it seemed awkward. And she didn't say anything as she walked away from him. Not a single, solitary word.

Yep. Had to be that kiss, he thought as he headed off to see his first patient. Then he smiled for the first time since it had happened. And what a kiss it had been.

Although it still didn't explain his attraction to the *last* person he should ever be attracted to. Maybe it was simply hormones, he decided as he veered into his first patient's room. Maybe a simple case of too long without a woman, then finally encountering the woman who'd always been able to push *those* buttons. He hoped so. Really hoped so, because horny he could explain. But something else… "Hello, Mr. Gardner. I see you had a rough night…"

* * *

OK, it wasn't a date. He had no reason to be nervous about it. But going out to Priscilla Anderson's was a long ride, so what the hell was he doing, taking Leanne along? This was an easy visit, one he could have made alone. But he'd passed her in the hall on his way out the door and next thing he knew she was sitting next to him in his truck, going along for the ride. Frankly, it had surprised him when he'd opened his mouth and heard the invitation fly out, but what surprised him even more was her acceptance. *Eager* acceptance.

Now here they were, bumping along a pitted mountain road, both probably wondering what had gotten them to this place. Especially considering the kiss—not the friendly one but the one that could have easily taken them straight down the hall to the bedroom. "So, did you know that, years ago, Victor Spencer at the hardware store got a little drunk and ended up on Betty Hollander's sofa? No one knew how he got there. She kept her doors locked and said she'd never given anyone the spare key. But she got up one morning, was in the process of getting ready to go to work and there he was, all sprawled out on her sofa in all his full, naked glory, snoring like he was king of the house. Or in other words... one of Marrell's interesting stories."

And a big, fat way to avoid real conversation, which was his only aim now.

"And I'm sure there are more."

"Many more," she agreed. "Deeper and more mysterious."

"Such as?" he asked, not twisting an inch to look at her, since to look at her was to wander off into dangerous territory, and he was too tired to wander. Or wonder.

"Such as why you asked me to come with you."

"Since when is it a crime to ask someone along on a ride?"

"It's not a crime. It's just...curious."

Finally, he glanced over at her. "As curious as your motive for accepting my offer?"

She laughed. "We really *are* good at going around in circles, aren't we?"

Caleb glanced at Leanne out of the corner of

his eye, and finally gave in to a smile. "And exactly what circles would those be?"

"Never thought I'd live to see the day," Priscilla Anderson said, leading Caleb and Leanne in through her door, past her many, many cats. "Caleb Carsten and Leanne Sinclair together. In my house, no less. You didn't take a detour through my *medicinal* patch the way you used to, did you?" she addressed Caleb, winking.

"You still have that thing?" Caleb sat his medical bag on the side table near the nineteen-sixties sofa, then turned to face the woman. She hadn't changed a bit. Long gray hair, sharp blue eyes, bright smile, faded blue jeans and a T-shirt sporting the peace sign. Somewhere well north of seventy, although he didn't know how much, as she'd always refused to tell anybody when they asked. *Age is in the mind, and my mind is young*, she'd always say. In fact, that's what she'd written into the medical information that was on file for her at the hospital.

"Maybe I do, maybe I don't," she said, this time addressing her wink to Leanne.

"Well, I was never interested in your *medicinals*, but I'd sure take a chocolate-chip cookie, since that's the only reason I came out here."

She reached up and tweaked his cheek. "If you're good, you can have as many as you like." Then she looked at Leanne. "Don't guess I ever expected to see you back here in Marrell, working."

Leanne shrugged. "Don't guess I ever expected to come back here to work. But things happen. And I'm only here until I get everything sorted at the hospital."

"Yes, Henry getting married and retiring," the older woman said, then broke into a wide grin. "To my daughter. Which makes you my granddaughter now, doesn't it?"

Leanne laughed. "I guess it would, wouldn't it?"

"Which makes you and my grandson Jack... cousins? I used to hope you and he might work something out. You seemed like a good couple. Well suited."

"We never dated, Priscilla. We weren't interested in each other that way. He was a friend.

He and his best friend, Palloton, taught me how to climb. That's all there was to it."

"I know, especially with what you and Caleb had going on," she said, then nodded toward Caleb, who'd found the cookies in the kitchen and was busy pouring himself a glass of milk to go with them.

"Nothing going on there either. Not then, not now."

"Well, there was that whole thing about you getting him arrested."

"I didn't get him arrested," Leanne protested, as she opened her medical bag and pulled out her stethoscope. If ever there was a person who spoke her mind, that was Priscilla. Usually, she didn't mind the bluntness. Right now, she did. It made her feel uneasy. Made her feel frustrated over something that just wasn't there. "He got *himself* arrested on his own."

"With a little help from a friend," Priscilla continued. "But true love makes you do crazy things, I suppose. Don't know for certain since my true love happened so long ago."

"It wasn't true love," Caleb called out from the kitchen.

"Are you sure?" she called back.

"Think I'd know it, if it happened to me," he teased, stepping back into her living room, cookie in hand.

"Or, maybe you wouldn't. For a genius kid, you weren't always too smart." She dismissed him with the wave of a hand, then turned to Leanne. "So, let's get this over with. Since Caleb's obviously not going to examine me while he's engaging with my cookies, and you've got the stethoscope, I'm assuming you're the one who's going to do it."

"In your bedroom?" Leanne asked.

Leanne followed Priscilla down the hall, entered the bedroom after her and shut the door. "OK, let's make this quick," she said, pointing to a vanity chair and instructing Priscilla to take a seat.

"You're not going to hurt him again, are you?" Priscilla asked, as she sat. "Because he doesn't deserve that. Didn't deserve it then, doesn't deserve it now."

"I don't know what you're talking about," Leanne said stiffly. Another accusation. This was really starting to bother her. What had these people seen in her they'd thought was so bad?

"Sure, you do. And you also know Caleb was one of the good kids in town. But you..." She shook her head. "Just leave him alone this time, Leanne. That's all I'm saying. Leave him alone to live his life the way he wants to. And I'm not trying to be mean about this. I'm just concerned."

"We weren't even friends back then, Priscilla. And I really don't have to stand here and defend whatever you think I did when I was a kid." Especially when it came to Caleb, since to her mind there was nothing to defend.

"He's a good man, Leanne. And I'm assuming you're a good woman. At least, that's what I hope you turned into. So just be careful this time. Whatever you two have going between you, just be careful with it." With that, she pulled up her shirt, then said, "So, examine me now, then you can go have some cookies, too, if Caleb hasn't eaten them all."

But she didn't want cookies. Didn't want anything but fresh air, which was exactly what she got as soon as she did her exam. She left Caleb to his cookies and went outside, sat down on the chair on Priscilla's porch and simply stared up at the sky, wondering why Priscilla Anderson would even think she needed to warn her about being careful with Caleb. How was that relevant? What did it mean? It didn't make sense. So many things didn't make sense that she was beginning to feel panicked, feel like something was missing. But what? For the life of her, she couldn't figure it out.

So, she shut her eyes, leaned her head back against the house, and simply breathed as she tried to shut out the conversation coming through the door she'd left ajar. But it wouldn't be shut out.

"All I'm saying is watch yourself, Caleb. She destroyed you once, and I don't want to see that happening again."

"She's my colleague, Priscilla. And, technically, my boss. That's all there is."

"That's never all there is, Caleb. Not back then, not now. You know it, and I know it. Probably half of Marrell knows it, too."

"You don't like Leanne, do you?"

"I don't like what she did to you. As for Leanne herself, I'm sure she's grown up, and now that we're going to be family, I suppose I'll get to know her differently. Hope so, anyway. But I've always cared a lot about you, Caleb. You know that. You weren't like the rest of the kids in town. And I just don't want to see all that come back to haunt you."

All what? Leanne wondered, letting out a frustrated breath. Exactly what would come back to haunt him?

CHAPTER SEVEN

"I'M SORRY, BUDDY, but I'm afraid it's just the two of us tonight." Caleb felt bad about that, as Matthew had his photos in queue on the computer, anxiously awaiting Leanne. But she'd called a while ago, told him she couldn't make it.

"Tell Matthew I'm sorry." No other explanation. She'd been edgy the whole time they'd been at Priscilla Anderson's earlier, which he understood since Priscilla and Leanne were not on the best of terms—something that seemed to have grown over the years, at least in Priscilla's mind. So, by the time he'd dropped Leanne off at her car, she'd looked as strung out as he'd ever seen anybody look, wringing her hands, biting her lower lip, anxiously tapping her foot, tense shoulders...

He'd felt sorry for her. Felt bad for asking her to go up to Priscilla's with him. But he'd honestly figured he could put everything out of his mind and simply get on with it. That didn't turn out to be the case, though. The closer he was to her, the more it all came back. So many memories, so many feelings— And Priscilla. She'd always hated Leanne's *influence* over him. Had told him, over and over, that she was no good for him, to leave her alone, to forget about her. Advice that always fell on the deaf ears of a teenager in love, lust or whatever it was he'd been in. And now the old lady was taking up the cause again—a cause he would have to take special care to keep Leanne away from. Although he wasn't sure why he felt compelled to protect her now. She'd been all those things Priscilla had accused her of being—spoiled, stuck on herself, out to use people, especially him...

And, yes, he was flirting with all that once more. Didn't mean to, didn't want to...couldn't even attach a rational explanation to it. But it was happening even though he didn't want it to. This time, though, he was older, not prone to getting himself hurt.

Except playing with fire always burned, didn't it?

"Look, Matthew, Leanne had…other things she had to do, so we'll show her your photos another time."

"But she was supposed to eat with us, too," Matthew said, sounding as disappointed as a five-year-old could sound.

"I know, but sometimes we have to change plans," Caleb said, sounding disappointed himself. Surprised how much he'd counted on this evening together. "Anyway, how about I go get dinner cooking?"

Matthew's answer was to shrug and sigh. "Not hungry," Matthew said. "I want to go outside and take some pictures."

"Want me to help?"

Matthew shook his head, then picked up his camera from the table next to the front door and walked on outside. Slowly. Hesitantly. Like an unsure little five-year-old boy. His son—still almost a baby, but so intellectually grown-up. Caleb felt so inadequate as a father, at times it almost pained him physically. Especially at times like this. "Stay in the yard," he warned. It was a small patch of earth, juxtaposed against a never-ending expanse of wilderness that he'd fenced off for Matthew's play area, even though his son rarely ever went outside to play.

"And later, I want to go online and look at cameras," Matthew said. "I need something with a better zoom."

Caleb didn't doubt Matthew would progress through the next level of camera, then the one after that very quickly, until he finally landed on a professional model. That's just the way he was. Always wanting to push the five-year-old boundaries far beyond those very limited years. It made him both proud because Matthew was so focused, yet sad for the things he might never see because of that focus. Much the way he'd been when he was young. Always focused on medicine, then Leanne...never seeing the world around him because he'd been centered *only* on what he'd wanted to see. "Do you think we should go to one of the bigger cities one day, and have a look in a camera shop? Talk to some experts, see what they recommend for you?"

"No," Matthew said, in a flat, I-have-no-interest-in-what-you're-saying voice. A voice Caleb knew, oh, so well. "I don't want to wait to get it." With that, Matthew shut the front door behind him, leaving Caleb standing there, feeling lousy. In fact, everything right now made him feel lousy. Leanne canceling her evening with them. His interactions with Matthew. And that damned fried chicken he was supposed to fix for them.

Matthew felt lousy, he felt lousy, Leanne felt lousy. It had been a hell of a lousy day all around.

"I'm going to get a new camera," Matthew said, aiming his camera at Leanne and clicking off several shots as she strolled up onto the front porch and took a seat next to him on the log bench. "I thought you weren't coming."

"Changed my mind. Decided I'd rather be here with you guys than home alone. And look at your photos." That was true, even after what she'd overheard at Priscilla's. Tonight, the emptiness at home, alone, hadn't suited her, and Priscilla's words had pounded and pounded. So much so, they made her do strange things. Think about things she hadn't thought about in years. Try to remember events, people, places…much of which had slipped her mind. Which had frustrated her. The harder she'd tried to think, to recall, the worse it had gotten until she'd literally stepped out onto the front porch and screamed her lungs out at the nighttime sky. Why not? No one was there to hear. No one was there to care. So, while she'd hoped for some sort of catharsis from it, all she'd got was a mild scratchy throat, a little bit of a headache, and the overwhelming feeling that she just didn't want to be alone. Wanted to be with Caleb. And, of course, Matthew. So, here she was, pulling out her phone and snapping a few pictures of Matthew taking pictures of her.

"They're ready," he said, turning his focus on a white-tailed deer crossing the front yard. "Got them in albums, ready to look at."

She waited for him to take his shot before she answered. "What kind of camera are you thinking about?" she asked him, taking a seat next to him.

"Can you help me with that?" He looked at the

camera she'd given him, and shrugged. "Some of the things I've read got me confused."

"Sure, I'll help you. There are a couple of brands I've always liked, so maybe after we look at your photos…" It was hard to believe she was talking to a young child this way, but this was Matthew, and to do anything otherwise would be to insult him. He was like Caleb, who'd used a lot of words, most of which she hadn't understood. But oh, how she'd loved to listen. At her young age, Caleb had been so impressive…like Matthew.

"I'm glad you came," Matthew said, jumping up and running to the edge of the porch to catch a photo of a jackrabbit running across the lawn.

"I am, too," she replied, watching him take his pictures. Trying so hard to be grown-up about it yet stomping his foot in a typical childish reaction when the rabbit scampered off before he got the picture he wanted. She really did enjoy spending time with Matthew. He almost put her in the frame of mind that she might, one day, want a child. *Almost.* "So, have you heard anything from Hans Schilling yet?"

"He's being too slow," Matthew said, changing his focus to a lone mule deer lingering at the edge of the woods, probably trying to decide if it was safe to leave its cover and head out across the open range.

"Well, I'm sure you'll hear something soon."

"Daddy says I may have to wait until I'm seven." Matthew said, his voice so solemn it almost sounded like Caleb. After taking several shots of the mule deer, which was alerted to the clicking of the camera and darted back into the woods, Matthew aimed his camera at Leanne like before, but instead of taking her picture again, he simply looked at her through its lens. "I don't think I'm too young, though."

"Don't give up on it, or yourself, Matthew. You never know what might happen."

"I might have to go live someplace else, where Daddy can find me a good teacher."

"Would you be OK with that?"

Matthew shrugged. "I like Marrell."

"Me, too, buddy," Caleb said from the doorway. "So, I think we'll probably stay here." He looked at Leanne, who was staring back at him, and gave her a nod and a wink.

Instantly, she jumped up and ran to hug Caleb, but stopped short. Another hug, another kiss… what was she thinking? Instead, she stopped short of him and whispered, "Really?"

Caleb gave her another wink, then said to Matthew, "Fried chicken on the table, with mashed potatoes and corn…not peas. Run upstairs and get washed."

"When did you find out?" she asked, once Matthew was gone.

"About twenty minutes ago."

"And you haven't already told him?"

"Not immediately, because he was disappointed that you weren't coming, and I didn't want that to ruin the news. And now that you're here, he's anxious to show you his photos, and I want him to have that moment before he has another. You know, keep him away from overload. Let him enjoy everything."

"I never meant to disappoint him. I figured my not being here wouldn't matter that much."

"He was counting on you, Leanne. You made

a promise, then you broke it. Young hearts get broken that way. But you're here now, and he's happy, and that's what counts." With that, he turned and went back into the house, leaving her to stand alone on the front porch for a minute, thinking about what Caleb had said about young hearts getting broken. He was right, of course, and those words…those simple words robbed her of her appetite. Made her feel as frustrated as she had when she'd come here a little while ago. Made her want to scream into the night again. But not because of all the pressures and uncertainties building up inside her. She wanted to scream because Caleb was happy that Matthew was happy. *Not because she was here.*

"So, my answer is finally yes. I'm going to accept that position at Sinclair," Caleb said casually, holding a glass full if iced tea in midair. "Going to buy this house and go from temporary to permanent status now."

"Well, at least that's one thing off my list." Matthew had eaten his dinner quickly, then rushed upstairs to add a few final touches to his queue of photos before he showed them to Leanne. She and Caleb were seated at the kitchen table, across from each other, in no hurry to get up or go anywhere. Not really hitting it off right now, but not *not* hitting it off either. "So, you'll tell him the good news after I leave?" She'd really hoped to be around for it, to see Matthew's excitement. But it wasn't hers to share, and she understood that. Still, it would have been nice...

"Probably tomorrow morning. Something his five-year-old brain can't do too well is process more than one thing at a time. Right now, he's excited about showing you his pictures, and if I tell him he's been accepted by Schilling, that will change his focus. He'll miss out on the one thing he really wanted to do this evening. So, I'll wait."

"You really do have some amazing insight into him," she said.

"Sometimes it keeps me up at night, trying to figure out how to stay one step ahead of him." He chuckled, and took a sip of his tea. "I suppose it was that way for my parents, too, since I was, well...academically gifted like Matthew."

"They say what goes around comes around. I suppose it's your turn now."

"He's a great kid. Best thing that's ever happened in my life because he gives me focus as much as I do the same for him."

"How are you going to deal with him living at the school and not with you?"

"Don't know yet. For a while I'll be miserable, I suppose. I know I'm going to miss his music… even when I don't physically see him, just hearing him play gives me a sense that all's right with the world. Not sure what I'm going to do without it, or him."

"Has he always played?"

Caleb nodded. "Pretty much. There was an old piano in the apartment we rented when I was still in the military. First time I heard him play it, he was two, picking out a simple melody from a cartoon he watched. One-handed, of course. But he was spot-on perfect. I already knew he was smart. Started talking early. Walked early. Well ahead of his normal developmental stage. I mean he had these little plastic letters…magnets, he would arrange on the refrigerator door.

Only by two, he wasn't just arranging random patterns like most kids do. He was spelling out simple words. The base psychologist ran him through some tests and told us we had a budding genius on our hands. Which, at the time, didn't mean a lot to me, as I'd assumed he could be smart and still be like other kids his age. Unfortunately, that wasn't the case. He wasn't on that level, didn't want to do the things two-year-old kids typically did."

"And your wife? How did she handle it?"

"I think Matthew's gifts were the proverbial straw that broke the camel's back in our marriage. She couldn't handle them. Didn't want to deal with the special arrangements we'd have to make to accommodate him. So, she left. Simple as that. Said married life and kids weren't what she wanted."

"And you?" Leanne asked.

"Learned by trial and error. Still learning." He smiled. "And keeping my fingers crossed a lot of the time."

Much the way her father had raised her. Trial and error, fingers crossed. Except Matthew was getting the attention from Caleb that she'd never gotten from her dad. He'd loved her. Just never had time for her. "No regrets?"

"One. I wasn't around much for Matthew's first two years. Spent a lot of time deployed to Afghanistan, and totally missed the baby phase of his life. Wish I could get it back, but I can't, so that's probably my biggest regret as far as being a dad. Now, if you want to talk about life regrets…"

Leanne laughed, then stood up. "I think what Matthew has lined up for me now takes priority. But, Caleb, just let me say, from what I see, you're doing an amazing job with him. I know it's tough, having been raised by a single dad myself, but he's a happy, well-adjusted little boy. Differently focused than most kids, but no worse for it. That shows hard work on your part."

"All I want is for him to fit in. Don't want him to be so different that the other kids pick on him the way they did me."

"That *can* be so damaging. And spill over into adulthood. I've read a lot of studies, even treated a few patients who have manifested adult symptoms of childhood bullying, and it's terrible. It's like they can never get rid of the nightmare. Which is why what you're doing for Matthew is so important. He doesn't deserve to have that happen to him."

Now he was frustrated. Even a little bit angry. How could she *not* understand? See, that was the thing about Leanne he just didn't get. On one hand, she was an open, insightful person who seemed to genuinely care. But on the other, she ignored a significant part of who she'd been. *The bully. The person who'd picked on him.* Maybe she wasn't that person now, but to deny what she'd been? Nope, he didn't understand that at all.

Didn't understand either why he was so damned attracted to her given his frustrations, anger and downright disbelief. But he was, which worried him as he'd always been blind about her back then, and he wondered if he was still that blind. "No, he doesn't. No kid does. But that's just what some kids do, Leanne. Don't you remember? Don't you remember high school?"

She frowned. "No one picked on me, Caleb. I got along with pretty much everybody."

"No. *You didn't*. But it was of your own choosing because *you* were the bully. *You* picked on kids who were different. You encouraged your friends to do it. You ridiculed other kids, called them names, laughed at them. Humiliated them. And I was one of them, Leanne. *You bullied me.*"

CHAPTER EIGHT

YOU BULLIED ME. Why couldn't she remember it? Her, the bully? That explained the light switch that went on and off with Caleb. But her memories of him were so ambiguous. He'd been a little different, and never a part of the group, yet he was always there. Hanging around. Still, he'd also been a troublemaker. At the time, probably the biggest one in Marrell, not that it had meant anything, as big trouble in Marrell hadn't been much by other standards. But back when they'd been kids, if there had been trouble in town, she remembered Caleb usually being a part of it.

But she didn't remember bullying him, and now she was scared. What was wrong with her? With her mind? With her memory? Caleb wasn't lying about it. She knew that, because of his reactions to her. Caleb might be a lot of things, but he wasn't a liar. Never had been.

So, if Caleb wasn't lying, why didn't she remember? How could she have been a bully when she hated everything that stood for? It went against her basic nature.

"Was I *that* bad to him, Dad?" she finally asked, plopping down in the chair across the desk from Henry. They were home, in his office, and she was hoping he had some answers for her, because she didn't have any—not even one. She probably should have talked it out with Caleb, but after he'd accused her, he'd walked away, shut himself up in his room, and left her there to look at photos with Matthew. Not that she remembered much of what she'd seen, she'd been so upset.

"Were you bad to him?" Henry repeated, shrugging. "Not so much when you were younger. In fact, I think you loved him as much as any little girl could love any little boy. And when you got older…" His face wrinkled into a frown. "I don't recall seeing anything that would indicate you were a bully. When you asked me if anything had gone on back then, I honestly tried to think back, but…" He shook his head. "At the time, I'd just absorbed John Wainright's practice into mine, and I was busy adding on some patient rooms, getting ready for my first expansion. So, I was pretty tied up. Probably not paying as much attention to you as I should."

That didn't surprise her. Her dad had never paid much attention to her. As fond as he'd been of Caleb, though, she was surprised he'd never noticed anything going on, at least on Caleb's side of it. "But he says I was a bully, Dad. So why would I have done that to him? And, most of all, not remember it?"

"I left you to your own devices too much. Maybe you were acting out to get attention. To be honest, there were a lot of times I gave Caleb more attention than I gave you. He always seemed so desperate to learn and, I think, to be someplace where he felt safe. Marrell was never safe for him. He was too smart. There was nothing here to stimulate him. And while his parents were…are good people, they were poor and couldn't afford a lot for their children. So, they worked all the time, trying to make ends meet.

Which left their kids free to wander around town all hours of the day and night."

"And you took him under your wing, while you ignored me. How was that supposed to make me feel?"

"At the time, I didn't know I was doing that. You had everything you could possibly want. You were popular with all the kids in town. I thought I was giving you a good life."

"You gave me *things*, Dad. You gave Caleb time." Was that why she'd bullied him? Because he'd had a part of her dad she'd never had, and she'd acted out in resentment?

"I did the best I could," Henry said.

"It hurt me, Dad. I deserved some of what you were giving Caleb and, yes, I resented that. Probably even hated him for it. But did I resent it enough to become a bully? And why don't I remember it?" There was something else, though. Something she could feel skulking around inside her. Gnawing. And she wanted to know what it was. Dear God, she wanted to know.

"Again, what can I say? I missed it, Leanne. Missed too much. But as for you hating Caleb, I always thought you had a crush on him. Didn't see any indications to the contrary."

"When I was young, Dad. When we were little kids. But I bullied him when we were older, and I don't remember it." The feeling of not knowing, not recalling was so frightening, she was getting nauseous. Her hands were shaking. She wanted her dad to wrap his arms around her and simply be her dad for a little while. Tell her he'd help her. Tell her it would be OK. But he didn't. Instead, he got up from his desk and walked to the office door, then laid his hand on it. He was walking away. As he'd always done.

"If you don't remember it, Leanne, it probably wasn't important." That's all he said, then he left. And she sat there alone, shaking, fighting back tears for the next ten minutes, trying to figure out what was happening to her. Or what had happened to her back then.

And feeling so, so alone it hurt.

Well, it hadn't come out the way he'd intended. Being blunt like that was not his style, and he certainly hadn't wanted to catch Leanne so off guard. But he had, and Caleb felt terrible about it. What purpose had it served, telling her how bad she'd been to him? She already knew it, even though she'd only hinted at vague memories of those days and had never truly owned up to them. Everybody in Marrell knew what those days had been like for him…for Leanne. The fact that he'd gone off the deep end and vandalized buildings up and down the main street after she'd humiliated him in front of half the town, then been hauled off to jail for it, hadn't exactly been a well-guarded secret. Or that he'd been sentenced to a year in juvenile detention as a result, and forced to finish off his schooling there.

But it had been three days now since they'd talked, and he didn't like watching Leanne do everything she could to avoid him. It was a small hospital in a small town, he worked for her, and ducking around corners or going in another direction could only go on so long before they'd finally have to confront the obvious. "I'm not sure what to do about it, Henry," he said, as the two of them sat at a table in the cafeteria, drinking coffee.

"She mentioned something about how badly she treated you," the older man said. "Seemed pretty upset about it."

"She should be. Leanne was…brutal."

"I think *she thinks* it happened because I paid more attention to you than I did to her."

Truth was, so did he. At the time, he hadn't caught on to that, but thinking back to those years, he didn't recall that Leanne had had much of a place in Henry's life. Which would explain a lot of things. But what it didn't explain was her refusal to either remember or admit it and, frankly, that had him stumped. More than that, it worried him.

What worried him even more, though, was that Matthew was caught up in this. Because no matter how it turned out between Leanne and him, Matthew had grown attached to her and if he couldn't trust her motives in hiding behind a *selective* memory, he couldn't trust her motives when it came to anything else. And that included Matthew. He was right there in the middle of this, and *he* was the one who needed to be protected. "Well, Henry, it sure as hell is complicated. I like Leanne, but I can't forget the way she treated me."

"She seems to have."

"I know. But she wasn't the one who spent a year in lockup because someone had bullied her into doing something bad. And that's a lot to live with."

"Well, I think, Caleb, that since you're going to be working for her, and she hasn't changed her mind about that, you two will have figure it out between you."

"Easier said than done," Caleb snapped. This was getting him nowhere. He was grumpy—didn't want to be. He was preoccupied—didn't want to be that either. And he was defensive—another thing he didn't want to be. All because Leanne wouldn't own up to it and Henry was oblivious to it. Also, because he was caught up in Leanne in ways he didn't want to be, or shouldn't be. But he was trapped. Had to stay in Marrell for Matthew. Had to work at the hospital because there was no place else for him to work. Had to tamp down his frustrations to be the best doctor he could be—with all this turmoil going on inside him.

Maybe, now that he'd declared his intentions here, Leanne would go back to Seattle, and he could get on with it. But she seemed reluctant about that now. Caleb blew out a frustrated breath. "Not sure what I'm going to do about this, Henry."

"Have you forgiven her for all that nonsense?"

"It *wasn't* nonsense. Innocent people were hurt. Mostly the people who associated with me. *And I was hurt.* Maybe I didn't realize it was such an issue then, but I do now, because every waking moment I worry about how Matthew will be accepted since he's a little different, the way I was. I worry that someone out there will bully him the way Leanne did me. Make fun of him. Coerce him into doing things because he simply wants to fit in. If this was just about me and some old feelings, it wouldn't be a big deal. But it's not. Because everything I went through…my son is likely to go through, too. And I'm just looking for a way to handle it better so I can be there for him if it does happen."

"Times were different then, Caleb. We weren't aware that being the victim of a bully could have such a bad effect."

"And in my day, it got me thrown in jail for a year. The army saved me, Henry. When no one else was there for me, I did the only thing I could think to do to give myself a chance at a decent future, and I would have stayed a soldier if I hadn't been wounded, because that's where I finally found myself and came to terms with the idea that I wasn't the one who caused the problem. Believe me, I spent a lot of time thinking I was. Unfortunately, Leanne hasn't come to terms with the fact that *she* was the one. And while I know she's not that person any longer, I really do have the right to know why. What happened? Was it me, was it her? What was it, Henry? What do I have to look out for with Matthew?"

"Talk her again, Caleb. And keep talking until she remembers it or admits it. If she bullied you, and you both seem to think she did, there's a reason and, yes, you do have the right to know. But don't hide behind Matthew as your excuse. You're the one who needs to know. It's about you, not your son. So, make it right with Leanne. And keep talking. Because you're never going to let yourself get truly settled here if you don't. And *that's* where Matthew will be affected. Not in what happened to you, but in how you're dealing with it right now."

"Talk to me about what?" Leanne asked, approaching the table. "How bad I was when I was a kid? How I ruined lives? I think I already know that."

Caleb rose to his feet and pulled out a chair for her, but she refused to sit. "I didn't mean to hurt you," he said, his voice low. "Didn't mean to just blurt it out like I did."

"What hurts, Caleb, is knowing that I hurt you. I've called a couple of old friends who said, yes, I was terrible to you. They told me a few things... not much. It's like I was so bad they can't talk about it. And since you won't..." She glanced over at her dad, who was trying to slip away unnoticed, then turned back to Caleb. "I need help. That's all I can think of. *I need help.*"

"Help, as in?" Caleb said, noting that Henry had finally made his exit.

"That's just it. I don't know." She shook her head. "I just don't know."

She looked so scared, so upset standing there, wrapping her arms around herself protectively. He really wanted to pull her into his arms, to hold her, to comfort her. But what he wanted and what he knew he should do were two different things. He was concerned, though, because for the first time he was beginning to believe she really didn't remember what had happened, that it wasn't a case of avoiding or rewriting it, as he'd thought she was doing. She was too upset, too genuinely upset to be doing that. "Have you had some kind of neurological injury in the past?" he asked.

She laughed bitterly. "That would be the simple way to explain it, but no. I haven't. And I'm really confused, Caleb," she confessed. "So much so I'm not even sure I should be practicing medicine right now. It kills me thinking that I could have hurt you...or others. I'm not like that, don't want to be like that. And I'm..." She swatted at a tear slipping down her cheek. "I'm sorry," she choked out. "So sorry."

Leanne turned and ran out the cafeteria door, while Caleb stood there and watched her. It didn't add up. Nothing about this added up.

Sighing, he grabbed his paper cup, still half-full of coffee, albeit now lukewarm instead of hot, and headed to his office, and his computer. There was definitely something going on with Leanne, and he wondered...

"We need to talk," Caleb said, poking his head in through Henry's office doorway. He was exhausted this morning, after pulling an all-nighter, doing research. But what'd he'd found—well worth the effort, he hoped.

Leanne spun around in her dad's chair to face him. "About what?"

She looked so totally defeated, so totally devastated, it broke his heart. "About you. About us."

"There is no us, Caleb. How could there be?"

"That's the question I keep asking myself, to be honest. But I like you, Leanne. The you who exists now. The you who existed when we were young. Not the interim you, though, during those

few teenaged years. Which is what I want to talk
to you about."

She sighed, and waved limply at the seat across
the desk from her. "Then talk. What else is left?
I took myself off active duty this morning, asked
Jack Hanson if he'd be willing to come to Marrell and cover for me for the rest of the time I
intended on being here. Then I resigned my position back in Seattle because I can't practice the
way I am. So, sure, talk. I've got all the time in
the world to listen."

"Are you sure you need to do all that? To go
from being so active to nothing...that's what happened to me when I was wounded, and it will
drive you crazy."

"Well, since I'm already half-crazy..."

"Maybe not," he said. "I'll admit, I'd wondered
if you were playing some kind of game with me,
or just trying to avoid something that's not pleasant to talk about...and then when you said you
didn't remember what you'd done to me, well,
let's just say I didn't buy into any of that either."

"Well, actually, I do remember some of it,
Caleb. The part where you're being handcuffed

and put in the back of the police car. And…" She shut her eyes, rubbed her forehead. "The look you gave me from the car window as they were taking you away. *I've always remembered that look, Caleb.* You were so…lost. Frightened. And hurt. Most of all, I remember you being hurt."

"I'd been hurt for a long time," he said, settling back into the chair. "But your dad said something to me yesterday that actually made sense. When I came back to Marrell and you were here, my defenses were raised. I'll admit that. But I kept telling myself it was because of Matthew. I thought I was angry that you wouldn't admit what you'd done, or simply wanted to avoid it, because I was trying to protect Matthew from having the same thing happen to him. But that's not the case, and your dad made me see that. I want to know, because I have a right to know. It's about me. Not my son. I'm putting him in a school where that won't happen to him, and I can't use him as my excuse. I need to know because *I* need to know."

"And I can't tell you. So, where does that get us?" She spun back around to face the window.

"I think it gets us to a place called childhood traumatic amnesia."

She didn't turn back to face him. "I already told you I didn't have a head injury, so how could I have amnesia?"

"Traumatic amnesia, Leanne. *Traumatic*. It doesn't come from an injury necessarily."

"And it doesn't manifest in adults, so what's your point?"

"The point is, maybe this is the place where the hero gets to rescue the damsel in distress."

Finally, she did turn around to face him. "Why do you even care? I mean, what's in it for you?"

The expression her face wasn't anger, though. It was futility, hopelessness. Heartbreak.

"Honestly, I don't know. Maybe a friend. Maybe more?"

"More? With someone who brutalized you? You don't want that, Caleb. How could you?"

That was the question for which he didn't have an answer. Maybe he was reaching back to the Leanne he'd known when they'd been young, or reaching out to the one she was now. Maybe he was even reaching for the one she'd been even when she'd bullied him. Because when it came to Leanne Sinclair, he'd never had a clear head. Not back then, not now. And there was nothing to hide behind with that reality. No way to account for it. No way to understand it. He'd always had feelings. The heart did what the heart did and sometimes there was no explanation. End of story. "What I want isn't very clear to me now, Leanne. Like your memory is not very clear to you."

"Because of this childhood traumatic amnesia."

"I think so. The chief symptom is you block out certain events that are just too difficult or traumatic to deal with. Sometimes it's associated with false memories, where you build sort of a fairy-tale story around it to make it better. Sometimes it's simply amnesia."

Suddenly, she was interested. It shone in her eyes. "Like post-traumatic stress syndrome?"

"Something like that. But childhood amnesia is, most often, a diagnosis related to a specific incident. Something that caused you to shut down. PTSD can take in a whole gamut of events."

"But I don't have a fairy-tale story that makes anything better, Caleb. I don't have anything."

"Which brings me back to what I originally said. Childhood traumatic amnesia."

"Which, like I said, is typical of younger children."

"Then maybe you're atypical. Who knows? Whatever the case, I think I'm onto something."

He hoped so. Dearly hoped so.

"Except I was never traumatized. Never subjected to anything harsh or cruel. No one ever hurt me. And I don't think my dad ignoring me is enough to cause it."

"Remains to be seen." The more he thought about it, the more he was positive he was right. Because that would explain so many things. Not *that* she'd bullied him, but why? To make things right between them, maybe even explore the feelings he was pretty sure he had, and hoped she had, they both needed to know. Then, once that was cleared up, well…he didn't know what came next but at least there were possibilities.

CHAPTER NINE

"WHY DO YOU want to do this?" Leanne asked Caleb. "Why do you want to spend the evening with me after what I've done to you, because I really don't even want to spend the evening with myself?" They were strolling along the banks of Miller's Pond, close to the edge of evening, when the sky was a cross between gold and blue. It was chilly, and she was grateful for the jacket he'd placed over her shoulders. Grateful for the solitude. Grateful he was still talking to her.

"Maybe because you connect me to something I haven't been connected to in a long, long time."

"I connect you to a difficult past, Caleb. And whether I'm suffering from this childhood amnesia you mentioned or not, it doesn't change the fact that, once upon a time, I'd have probably shoved you in the pond rather than walk with you beside it."

He chuckled, then stepped closer to her when she shivered, and wrapped his arm around her shoulder. "I'm sure you would have."

"So, why bother with me? You're a nice guy. Good-looking. Smart." She reached across her left shoulder with her right hand and took hold of his hand. "Why drag someone up out of your past who hurt you, when you could be moving forward?"

"You think I'm good-looking?" he asked.

She turned to look at him. He was better than good-looking. In fact, he might have been the most handsome man she'd ever known. Beautiful eyes. The most kissable lips... A toned body that proved he treated it with discipline and care. She'd never been attracted to the cowboy-type before. In fact, she'd never had a type. But Caleb...he was different, and her attraction to the physical side of him was so keen she was afraid it would show on her. Her attraction to the deeper man was so much more than that, though, and that's what scared her as while she could handle the physical, she'd never had to think beyond that. *Not with any man.* Never had to react beyond that.

And now that's all she wanted. But couldn't have because, in the end, could he really ever forgive her? *Or trust her?* He was being nice now, because that's who he was, but it would wear off. She was as sure of that as she was unsure of herself. "You grew up well," she conceded, willing her heart to beat a little slower, her breaths to come a little easier. "Filled out."

"I was kind of a gawky kid, wasn't I?"

"You were," she said, as an image of him returned to her. Always taller than the other boys his age. A good ten pounds lighter than most. Glasses that had always been askew. Hair that had stuck out. "So, what happened that you changed into—well, what you are now?" Trite conversation, when she really wanted to dig deeper. But it was safe, and for now safe was good enough.

"Part of it was the army. It put muscles on me. Some of it was just the growing-up process—I started to care what I looked like. Could afford better clothes. And most of it was looking in the mirror at the odd reflection that looked back. I didn't like him very much. He was a troubled kid, a bad kid. I didn't want to be him anymore."

She pulled away from him, bent down and picked up a rock, a palm-sized flat one, and handed it to him.

"Do you remember that?" he asked. "How I used to come down here and spend hours skipping rocks on the water? I tried to teach you once, and you got impatient because you couldn't do it. Told me I was a horrible teacher."

"You were," she said, pulling his jacket tighter around her. "But in your defense, you were only, what? Seven or eight?"

He adjusted the rock in his hand, cocked back his arm, and gave it a lob into the water, then watched it skip across the surface several times, leaving circular ripples in its wake. "However old I was, I thought I was pretty good. But, then, I was a little distracted."

"By what?" she asked.

"You. You *always* distracted me, Leanne. Even when I was that age."

It should have surprised her, but it didn't because there were several images of him just being there that were trying to pop through. So many times, when they'd been together, doing just this. Taking a walk. Skipping rocks. Doing nothing yet having fun.

"Chemistry's chemistry," he said, smiling. "When you're young, who knows what it is? Mutual interests, maybe? Then when you're older it turns into a battle of the hormones. You're not old enough to be smart about the girl you pick out, so you let your hormones do the talking. At least, that's the way it is for a lot of guys."

"And your *hormones* chose me?" Somehow, she was a little disappointed to hear him say that. She'd really wanted to hear...well, he'd hung around for some other reason. Her intelligence. Her wit. Her compassion. But maybe she'd never shown any of that to Caleb. Maybe he'd never known that side of her existed, he had been so bombarded by *hormones*.

"You were the prettiest girl in Marrell. I wasn't the only one with hormones choosing you." He chuckled. "In some ways, that kind of innocence is nice. You conjure up these fantasies that you're sure will work out, if only you get the chance…"

"My fantasy was to get out of Marrell. I didn't want anything connecting me to it, anything that could pull me back to it. So, what was your fantasy?"

"Normalcy, I think. Not to be singled out for being too smart, or picked on for being too geeky. Took me a long time, and a lot of twisted roads to get there, but I did."

"Which means you're happy in Marrell?"

"Which means it's not about the place. I'm not sure I even realized it a few weeks ago when I moved back. But when you love someone more than you love yourself, your fantasy gets tied up in doing everything you can for her or, in my case, him."

"Personally, I think happiness is overrated," she said, then walked on ahead, up the trail. Not so much because she wanted to get away from him as she wanted to get away from the conversation. Because, for the first time in her life, she wondered if she'd ever been truly happy anywhere, with anyone, for any reason. She didn't know, couldn't remember. Couldn't pass it off on childhood amnesia either.

"Why?" he called out to her, hurrying to catch up.

"I get restless because I don't ever get happy," she said, when he finally caught up to her. "Restless with where I am, with the people I'm with. With life. With love. All of it. I always ask myself—is that all there is? Then I get disappointed when I find out it is."

He reached out, took hold of her arm and stopped her. Then twisted himself until he was facing her. "You used to tell me I was boring. But I wasn't, Leanne. I was probably the most active kid in town. Sometimes not active in the right direction, but I was never boring. I think, though, it was you who was boring. I just didn't realize it at the time because…"

"Of your hormones," she supplied, smiling.

"They *were* pretty intense."

She sighed. "Well, you're right. I was boring. Predictable, too."

"You remember that?"

"What I remember is that every day, when I

woke up, the boundaries of Marrell seemed a little smaller. And nothing changed except the feeling that I was getting squeezed in. By the town, by my dad, by always being so…alone." She looked up at him. "I was frustrated and angry and I took it out on you, because you made yourself vulnerable to me. At least, that's my theory."

"I was in love with you, if a kid that age can actually be in love. Thinking back, it may have been more about teenaged lust, but at the time… I didn't know. I just had these crazy feelings that kept me coming back. Can't explain them, don't understand them, don't even want to."

Leanne looked up at Caleb, brushed his cheek with her hand. "I'm so sorry you did," she whispered, then turned and ran from him. Because to stay was to start down yet another path in her life. One where she might have wanted what Caleb wanted, yet one she knew would make her restless, as it always had before. And, yes, she did remember that. Vividly.

"Running away doesn't fix things," he called out, even though he stood still. Didn't attempt to go after her. "I did that for a while after I started to understand that my life was forever changed. I couldn't be a surgeon. Couldn't be a husband. So, I took Matthew and disappeared for a time. A few months here, a few weeks there. Then I stopped off in Las Vegas, stayed for a while and look where I am now."

"But you're not me," she said, stopping about a hundred yards up the path and then turning to face him. "You had a goal. I don't. For you, it's been about your son. For me, it's been about—me. Big difference, there, Caleb. You have someone in your life who counts. I have…" Her voice trailed off because there was nothing to say. She had no one.

"You have your dad, even though that relationship is a little rocky. And you have a hospital. There are also people in town who'd love to see you come home and stay."

"Which isn't enough. Nothing's ever been enough, Caleb. My job. Eric. Living in Marrell. What difference does any of it really make?"

He started to walk up the path toward her, but stopped halfway. "That would be a question you have to answer. In my life I found my answer, which is why I can live here again. And even be happy. It's all about having someone to live for."

"Maybe," she said. "But maybe some people aren't meant to be happy, no matter what's going on in their lives." She hadn't used to be so cynical, so pessimistic, but something was chewing at her, dragging her down. And Caleb seemed to be a reminder of everything she didn't understand. It was frustrating. "I don't have any place to look for answers the way you do."

"You look inside yourself, Leanne. I didn't when I was a kid, when you were being brutal to me. I wasn't mature enough. But after I became an adult, when everything in my life changed, I had to find my way back or find something new. And there was nobody out there pointing me in the right direction. I had to find it, and acknowledge it on my own."

"Was I *that* brutal, Caleb?" A part of her wanted to know, yet a part of her didn't. And she was feeling so discouraged, so emotionally tired, all she wanted to do was drop to her knees in the middle of the path and cry. But that would leave Caleb to pick her up, and she didn't want that because she truly didn't want to hurt him again, or involve him in her life in a way that risked disappointment and failure. And that's all she felt right now…disappointment and failure.

"Not all the time. Especially when we were younger. But as we got older…yes, it was brutal. I was an easy target for you and you took advantage of that."

She sighed heavily. Shook her head, brushed back the tears that were welling in her eyes. "Why would *that* cause childhood amnesia when you were the one being traumatized?"

He started walking toward her again, and when he caught up he simply stood in front of her. No effort to get close. No effort to touch. "I'd like to think you blocked it out because you didn't like being that way. But that's just me, and a whole lot of wishful thinking. Maybe it was about you being unhappy with just about everything in your life, and I was the convenient scapegoat. The people closest to us are often the easiest to pick on, and we *were* close for a lot of years."

No. That wasn't it. She *knew* that wasn't it. "I'm considering counseling. Actually, I've decided to do it when I go home. No more speculations, Caleb. *I have to know.* But on my own. Not from anybody else." She stretched up and kissed him lightly on the lips. A lingering kiss, with just the tiniest flicker of passion. Snaked her hand around his neck to hold him there even when the kiss ended, and looked straight into his eyes. "Whatever happens, you're being a lot nicer to me than I probably deserve." And maybe they could start again, with a real beginning. She hoped so. Because she cared for him so deeply, and in Caleb she saw a flicker of hope, maybe the first one in her life.

But the reality was, maybe this couldn't be fixed. She didn't know because…*she still didn't know.* And that's what bothered her the most. Something was badly broken, something that needed to be fixed, and she didn't know what it was.

As she began to lower her hand, he caught her hand and held it against his cheek. "We all have things we don't like about ourselves."

"But what I don't like about myself is what I did to you. And you won't tell me what it was, will you?"

"Not the specifics," he said, kissing the palm of her hand. "I spent a lot of time trying to get past it. Broke windows on half a city block because of it. Set fires. Went to jail. Joined the army. There's nothing about any of that I want to relive."

"Yet you've forgiven me." Finally, she pulled her hand away, yet when she dropped it to her side he took hold of it.

"No, I haven't."

She blinked her surprise. Jerked completely away from him. "But I thought…"

"You thought I was over it. But what you did… it changed my life. For a long time, and not for the better. I've moved beyond that, found something that gives my life real significance. But you hurt a fundamental part of me, Leanne, and it turned me into a different person for a long time. I like who you are now. More than I ever thought I would. In fact, there's a possibility that I'm falling in love with you again…and don't ask me to explain that because I can't. But the bottom line is I'm not over who you were back then."

Now her head was spinning. She didn't know what to do. What to say. "I'm…um… I'm going back to Seattle first thing tomorrow. I think it's for the best." The pain of rejection…it was stabbing her now. Not the way it had when her dad had rejected her. Or Eric. It was a different pain. One that robbed her of the tiniest vestige of the hope she was desperately clinging to. One that left her numb. Was this how Caleb had felt all along? Was this what she'd done to him? Dear God, she hoped not, because what she was feeling right now was the very definition of falling into the pit of despair. It was deep, and she didn't know if she could, or even wanted, to climb out. Not if Caleb couldn't forgive her.

Three weeks. Three long weeks, and this was the first time he'd had to kick back and relax. *Alone*. Leanne was gone. Back to Seattle, maybe back to her old job—he didn't know since his few attempts to get in touch with her had failed. No responses to texts, phone calls, emails… After about a week of that he'd stopped trying.

The next move, if there was to be one, had to be hers.

And Matthew. He'd settled into Schilling's school a week ago. Caleb stopped by every day to see him, but it wasn't the same as having his son home, and he was filled with all kinds of doubt and guilt, letting his five-year-old son live at a boarding school. But Matthew was happy so far. He loved practicing on a concert grand, loved that his schedule was centered around his music, loved the horses in the stable, loved taking pictures of everything and posting them to the internet. He was fitting in, too, despite the age difference between him and most of the other kids, because this was a place where kids like Matthew had control of their world. There were no bullies. There were no threats. Best of all, Caleb didn't have to worry continuously about how his square-peg son would fit into the round-hole world, because at Schilling's he fit in beautifully.

But he missed Matthew. The nights seemed so empty and long. And lonely. It amazed him how one little boy took up so much space in his life. On nights like these, though, when he missed him to the point of aching, he did find some comfort in knowing that Matthew was happy. In his life, that's what mattered most.

But Leanne mattered, too, and he missed her. Didn't want to, didn't mean to. But he did. So, sinking down into his leather sofa, with a bottle of beer in one hand and his cell phone in the other, he considered calling her again. Just to hear her voice on the voice mail. He'd done that a couple times. Made the call knowing she wouldn't pick up or call back. Hoping these stupid feelings would go away. But they didn't. In fact, as the days dragged on, they only intensified.

Caleb sighed, kicked off his boots and shut his eyes, hoping he could rid himself of her image just this one night. What he wanted was to drink his beer, clear his mind and breathe. What he got, though, was a phone call from Hans Schilling.

Matthew was missing.

It was six hours into the search and practically everybody in Marrell was out looking for Matthew. And while Caleb was trying to present a cool, collected and optimistic front, he was falling to pieces inside. He'd been on foot for all of those six hours, stumbling around in the dark, like so many people were, knowing that he could practically step right over his son and not see him. No moon, no stars tonight. It was dreary, overcast, threatening rain. So far, it was holding off, but for how long?

"Drink the coffee, rest for an hour, then go back," Henry instructed him, as Caleb dragged himself back into the hospital cafeteria a little after midnight. This was where they'd set up the search and rescue headquarters, where people were gathered, waiting for news, trying to be helpful. Where his mom and dad and grandmother were huddled off in a corner, clinging to each other, trying to put on a brave front—a front he himself could not put on because there was nothing brave about him tonight. He was scared to death. Worse than he'd been when he'd been arrested that night. Worse than he'd been when he'd almost died on the battlefield.

"Can't rest. Got to get back out there," Caleb said, giving a weary sigh. "I'll take a coffee to go, but…" The urge to scream was closing in around him. Scream, cry…it all had to wait. He had to go find Matthew because even these few minutes away were killing him.

"But what, Caleb?" Henry asked him. "Seriously, it's going on to 1:00 a.m. People are coming back in now. They need to rest before they go back out tomorrow." He laid a comforting hand on Caleb's shoulder, but Caleb shook it off. "You need to rest, too."

"I can't, Henry. I have to…" He stopped, shook his head, steadied himself with a deep breath before his emotions got the best of him. "I have to be out there, doing something. I can't just sit around here, waiting." Feeling helpless and hopeless.

"Everybody in town is doing what they can," Henry reassured him.

"I know, and I appreciate that. But I'm his dad. I have to do more." He glanced across the room at Hans Schilling, who was beside himself with worry. Under different circumstances, he might have tried to comfort the man, told him it wasn't his fault that Matthew had disappeared from under his care. But he wasn't feeling that sympathetic or generous yet. Wasn't feeling anything except numb. "Look, I'll take that coffee with me, but I'm not going to hang around. I'm heading back to my cabin to see if he's shown up there, then I'm going to walk the road from there over to Schilling's school again. Matthew knows that route, so he could he heading one way or the other."

"I hope he is, son." Henry glanced over at Dora, who was pouring the coffee for Caleb, then glanced back at Caleb. "If he hasn't shown up by morning, Dora and I are going to take the boat out on the river...not that we think he might be down there but that will give us a different vantage point, and maybe we'll see something on the shoreline."

Caleb didn't even want to think in terms of Matthew being anywhere near the water, but he knew that, at some point, they'd have to look at that as a real possibility. He wasn't ready, though. Not yet. "I appreciate that," he said, taking the coffee from Dora, then heading out of the caf-eteria to the hospital's front door, where the always stolid Helen McBriarty wiped tears from her eyes and gave him a hug. No words spoken, just a hug. And he appreciated that. Appreciated all the hugs he'd received in the past hours, and all the good wishes, and all the promises to help. For the first time in his life, Marrell felt like it was home to him. A real home. For him, and Matthew...

"Sorry I didn't get here sooner," Leanne said. She ran straight to Caleb and threw her arms around him as soon as he approached his truck. "I chartered a plane and flew in as soon as I could after I got your message. Caleb, I..." She hugged him tighter. "What can I do?" she whispered.

He hugged her back, harder than he'd ever hugged anybody in his life. Glad for the feel of her, the comfort of her. "Thanks," he choked, on the verge of breaking down. "I wasn't sure you'd come."

"How could I not? I love that little boy, Caleb. And I love you, which is complicated, and confusing, and this isn't the time to talk about it. But this is where I *have* to be." She brushed tears from her eyes. "With you."

"I've missed you," he said, relaxing into her. Just having her there made things better. Made him feel…hopeful.

"I've missed you, too, and I'm sorry this is what brought me back. Sorry I haven't kept in touch, but…" She sniffled. "So, what happened? How did he disappear?"

"Nobody's sure. He was around all day, went to all his classes, hung out with some of his friends. But then he didn't show up for dinner. Several of the instructors went looking…he just wasn't there."

"Which was how long ago?"

"Almost seven hours. They called me as soon as they knew he was missing, and I've been out hunting ever since."

"Did he take his jacket?"

"No. It was still in his room when I looked. And he's so small…hypothermia. Wild animals, cliffs, the river, God only knows what else…"

Leanne took him by the hand and led him to the passenger's side of the truck, opened the door for him, then laid her hand on his chest. "Stay positive, Caleb. There are a lot of places in the woods to hunker down for the night, and when Matthew gets too cold, I'm sure he'll figure that out. Or has already figured it out. And the animals...we both know that unless he bothers them, they'll probably shy away from him. No one that I can recall has ever been attacked by a wolf or anything else around here. So..." She gestured to the seat. "Get in. I'll drive."

"To where?"

"Wherever you want to go. No arguments. Let me help you do this."

"No arguments," he said, climbing in.

She did likewise on the driver's side, but before they took off she turned to him, brushed her hand across his cheek and said, "When this is over, when Matthew is back home, safe and sound...we need to talk."

He nodded. "I know."

"So, where are we headed?"

"Back to my cabin first. Then I want to walk the road to the school."

"Did he take his camera, Caleb?" she asked.

"I don't know. I should have looked, but I didn't think about it." He'd been too frantic. In too much of a hurry.

"Then let's stop at the school first. Because if he took his camera…he texted me yesterday about some places he wanted to get pictures of. I told him we would, as soon as I got back to Marrell."

"You texted him?" Caleb asked, quite surprised. Also, quite surprised she'd told Matthew she was coming back.

"Of course I did. Pretty much every day. Looked at some of the photos he was sending me, too. Which is why I think we need to find out if he took his camera. Because if he did, he had a specific destination in mind."

Caleb blew out an anxious breath. "Which means you might know where he is."

"Which means I might know one of the ten places he wanted to go."

Too much to hope for. Too much to hang on to. But it's all he had. That, and Leanne. And he wasn't sure about any of it right now.

* * *

"It's not here," Caleb said, crawling out from under Matthew's bed, empty-handed.

"I called Hans Schilling and he told me one of the little girls said Matthew likes to go out in the evenings, just before dinner, and take pictures. She said he likes the sky."

Caleb stood, took one more look around Matthew's room and stepped over to the desk. "Do you think he might have downloaded something onto his computer that would give us a clue?"

"Give me a second," Leanne said, sitting down at the desk and flipping open Matthew's laptop. "He's using the photo editing program I bought him, so..." She clicked a couple of commands and popped right into the site where Matthew's photos were stored, and there were hundreds of them. "Looks like he's been busy." She clicked into the folder that seemed to hold his latest photos, and started to scan through them, until she came to one that caught her attention so much she enlarged it. "It's an eagle," she said. "Light angle shows it's near dusk. He's got all these photos, but..." Leanne went quiet and scrolled quickly to a very long slide show of nothing but eagle shots. "Six days, Caleb. He's been shooting this eagle for six days straight."

"From the same place?" he asked anxiously.

"No. It's mostly a sky shot, but I can see some treetops in the background, and it looks to me like he's tracking it from a different place each time." She looked up. "Getting closer, each time, to the trees. I think he's trying to follow it back to its nest." She took one more look, then turned off the laptop. "It may be the same bird, Caleb. I think he's onto her nocturnal pattern, and that's why he goes outside with his camera every evening before dinner. He wants to get closer to her. Wants to get her in her nest. Like we talked to him about that day, going up to—"

"Eagle Pointe?" Caleb gasped. "But that was the first place we searched."

"And the next," she said. Leanne stood up, walked over to the window and looked outside. "But going back up there now…" She closed her eyes to visualize Eagle Pointe. He *had* to be there. It was the place he'd associate with the nest. The nest, the vantage point… *The vantage point.* She sucked in a sharp breath. "Do you remember Devil's Cave?" she asked. Named as such because it was said that only the devil himself could get down to it. The devil, or someone such as herself, with the climbing skills it took.

Caleb cringed. "Yes," he said, his voice on edge. "You used to take a rope, and it was a sharp, steep drop over the edge. What was it, about twelve or fifteen feet down?"

"Probably more. And for a photographer it's the best vantage point if you want a good shot of the eagle's nest over on the opposite ridge. It puts you almost up inside the nest, it's so close."

"He couldn't have gotten down there," Caleb said. "It's too far. There's no path."

"But we all used to do it. Use to go up past Priscilla's, then hide out in the cave to smoke because we didn't think anyone would ever find us there since most people wouldn't make that climb."

"I wasn't one of those kids, Leanne. I didn't go down to that cave with you. I wasn't a climber. At least, not like you were. Didn't want to embarrass myself in front of you."

She gave him a puzzled look. "Sure, you were. I remember you being down there." She had a vivid impression of him there. Saw it as clearly as she saw him standing there with her. "You, me, Scott…some of the others."

"No," he insisted. "I didn't go down there with you. *Ever.*"

Well, she certainly didn't understand that, because she *did* remember him there—one of the few things she truly remembered from back then. But now wasn't the time to talk about it. Especially not if Matthew might be down there. "Matthew could be there, Caleb. If everybody's already looked around the trail, then the cave…"

"He would have fallen," he said, his voice so quiet she could barely hear him. "He might have scooted on his belly to get himself as close to the edge as possible, but it would have been almost dark, and he might not have seen the sharp dropoff. And since we didn't go all the way up there with him that day, he'd have no way of knowing…"

Leanne turned away from the window, stared at Caleb for just a second. then broke into a dead run out the door and straight to Caleb's truck. By the time she got herself into the driver's seat, he was in next to her. And neither one of them spoke for that interminably long drive to Eagle Pointe.

But when they finally did arrive, Leanne held back at the truck. If Matthew went over the edge, they needed help. Needed more than she and Caleb could do together. "You go on up, and I'll be right behind you. I'm going to let my dad know where we are, and have him get some other people up here to help us."

Rather than answering her, Caleb grabbed hold of Leanne's shoulders, gave her a quick kiss on the mouth, then headed straight up the trail to the top of the point. And Leanne, as it turned out, was only steps behind him as she'd discovered there was no cell reception in the area. When she got to the top, she stopped short of Caleb, who was down on his hands and knees, shining his flashlight down below, trying to scan the small ledge at the mouth of the cave.

"He's not there," he said. "Which means, if he

did fall, he either crawled into the cave or missed the ledge altogether…"

"He's in the cave," she said. Not that she knew. But it's what she hoped. Because if he'd missed hitting the ledge and fallen on down—Dear God, she didn't even want to think about that because no one could survive that fall. "Do you have a rope in the truck?" she asked.

"In the bed. Under a tarp."

She nodded, her mind still swirling with all the awful possibilities, then blew out a jagged breath. "I'll be back in a few minutes." As she descended the trail back to the truck, she heard Caleb calling out Matthew's name. Over and over. But as she came back up with the rope, it was quiet. Too quiet. And when she got to the top—Caleb wasn't there.

"Caleb!" she cried. "Matthew!" No answer. So, she moved closer to the edge. "Caleb! Can you hear me?"

When he didn't answer again, she got down on her hands and knees and crawled over to the edge, taking care not to put her weight down on one of the serrated, unsupported overhangs that fringed the entire span of the view down. And that's when she saw him. Caleb. On the cave ledge. Sprawled out, flat on his face.

Not moving.

CHAPTER TEN

LEANNE WAS IN Caleb's truck, pushing the speed as far as it was safe to do, heading back to town, continually pulling over, punching buttons on her phone, hoping to get reception, then moving on when she didn't. Try after try, no bars, nothing. She was desperate to hear her dad's voice on the other end. Desperate to get help up to Eagle Pointe. And more desperate than anything not to have to leave Caleb behind. And Matthew... if he was inside the cave.

And daylight...she was desperate for that, too. But it wasn't yet two, and whatever happened to rescue Caleb would be done in the dark. Which scared her, as nobody in Marrell, to her knowledge, was qualified to do that kind of rescue. And like it or not, she was probably the best climber in the area, next to Jack Hanson, who was on his way in from Phoenix but not here yet. Which meant…

Suddenly an image of Eagle Point flashed its way past her memory. It was at night. *That night.* Everybody was there. Including Caleb. All the kids from town. Doing things they shouldn't be doing. Partying. Drinking. And… Her stomach knotted. Her breath caught in her lungs. The image disappeared.

Leanne pulled over yet again, tried her phone again, and clicked it off once more when she got nothing. *Except another flash.* Caleb. Talking to Scott. The two of them looking at her. Laughing. *She could see it.* But why that image? Why was *that* returning? And now? Caleb… Scott… The image stayed there as she continued toward town. It was poking her now. Not staying flat but coming to life. Springing out, grabbing, clutching her, choking her… And she was getting lightheaded. Her breathing labored. So, she pulled over again, punched in her dad's phone number once more. Tried to catch her breath. Tried to calm the panic attack that was trying to take her.

Then, suddenly, all she could see was her

anger. Red. Furious. And directed at Caleb. She *wanted* to hurt him. *Wanted* him to hurt the way she did, because he hadn't turned out to be her friend the way she'd always thought he was. Because… "Oh, no," she whispered, as her hands started to shake, and the floodgate of memories opened. "Oh…no. *No*."

"Hello? Leanne?" a familiar voice crackled over the phone, breaking into her thoughts. "Is that you, Leanne?"

She slapped at the tear sliding down her cheek, then shook her head to stop the dam that had just burst. "I'm in Marrell, Dad. Came in a little while ago. And I have an injury out here. I need help. Caleb's been injured. He might be…"

"What are *you* doing up here?" she asked her dad, who'd trekked up the mountain path with a dozen others.

"I may be old, but I've done this more than you have." He was carrying a backpack full of medical supplies, which he handed over to Leanne. He stopped near the edge and shone his flashlight down. "Any signs of life?"

She shook her head. "It's been half an hour, and Caleb hasn't stirred. I've been calling for Matthew, but if he's in the cave, he's either too afraid to call back or he's hurt, too." She slung the pack over her shoulder and headed to the edge of the cliff, where a rope was being tied off for her. To her knowledge, this was the first time she'd ever *really* worked with her dad.

"You sure you want to be the one to go over?" he asked her. "A couple of the men up here are pretty experienced climbers."

"Not as good as me, Dad." But he probably didn't know that. Hadn't paid attention during that summer Jack Hanson had taught her. "And since I've got the medical background…" She gave her dad a quick hug and got herself into position to be lowered. "Who's minding the hospital, by the way?"

"Dora. And Jack will be here shortly. He's about an hour out, last time I heard."

"Good. Too bad he didn't make it in time to go down with me." She cinched in, and backed all the way to the edge. Took a deep breath, then lowered herself. All the while facing her returning memories as she climbed. The last time she'd climbed down there had been *that* night. Caleb had gone down, she didn't know why. Didn't care. Hadn't cared then. In fact, all she'd cared about had been getting down there with a couple of friends following her, and to humiliate him. Betray him the way he'd betrayed her. Or betrayed, from a teenager's perspective.

Now she was going down to rescue him.

Luckily, twelve feet didn't take any time to scale, and within a minute she was kneeling alongside Caleb, feeling for a pulse. Thanks heavens it was strong. But his face...his beautiful face was all bashed. Cuts, bruises, what looked to be a broken cheekbone. And his shoulder... the one he'd injured before. Definitely broken. "You're in rough shape," she said, as her hands skimmed the rest of his body in a quick assessment. Legs seemed fine. Belly wasn't distended or rigid, so he might have escaped internal injuries. Pupils equal and reactive. "But you're stable, and I've got a litter on the way down to pull you back up top."

Except she had to go and see if Matthew was

in the cave before she strapped Caleb in, because if Matthew needed to be out of here first... "Don't know if you can hear me, but I'm going to look for Matthew." She picked up his hand and brushed a light kiss to it. "Just don't move, Caleb. Listen to me. *Do not move*. And, please, trust me. No matter what I've done, no matter what I've said in the past, trust me now."

She waved up to one of the rescuers who was on his way down to stay with Caleb. Then grabbed her backpack, darted into the darkness of the cave, turned on her light and started to navigate the narrow passageway toward the back. It wasn't a very wide cave but it was deep. And she hesitated before she proceeded. "You can do this," she whispered. "You've got to do this..." She blew out a hard breath and fought back the nausea trying to rise in her. Not because she feared the cave. She didn't. But because she feared what she might find in it. "For Matthew," she said, then took a step, then another. Stopped. Steadied herself against the passage wall, and the horrible memories trying to push her back, and called out to Matthew again. Her voice was so unsteady, she didn't even recognize it as it bounced along in front of her. "I'm coming after you." Fighting unwilling legs. Fighting clear thoughts of what had happened. To Caleb. *And to her.*

"Matthew? Are you here?" Her voice echoed back through the chamber, but that's all she heard. So, she kept going forward, kept looking. Shining her light. Shivering against the chill. Struggling against the mental avalanche that was threatening to bury her alive if she let it. "Matthew…" But she wouldn't let it. She was stronger than that. Finally, stronger now that she knew. And she had two people she loved who needed her help. "Can you make a noise so I'll know where to look?" she called out.

But he didn't, and her next minute was filled with starts and stops, listening, moving on. Then, after what seemed an eternity but which her logical brain told her had only been a few minutes, she stumbled over something in the passage and fell to her knees. Before she righted herself, she flashed her light over the passage floor, and that's when she saw it. A camera lens. It had rolled off to the side and she'd almost missed it. But it was there. And Matthew was, too, somewhere.

Scrambling to her knees, Leanne pushed herself up to standing, doubled her speed and continued toward the back, where the narrow passage closed into a belly-crawling tunnel for about fifty feet, then opened into a large chamber. *A chamber she knew.* The chamber where she'd watched her friends strip Caleb naked, at her urging, then leave him there without a rope to climb out. The chamber where Matthew had to be.

And he was there. After her belly crawl, pushing her backpack along in front of her, she reached the end of the tunnel, and even before she was out of it, her flashlight captured Matthew huddled in a fetal ball, rocking back and forth, whimpering.

Thank God.

"I broke my camera," he sniffled, as she crawled up to him.

She made a quick assessment and discovered he was fine. Cut up, banged up and bruised. Scared. Cold. But fine. Her response was to grab him up in her arms and simply hold him close.

"We'll get you another one," she promised, as tears streaked down her cheeks. "We'll get you another one."

He hated it here. Hated the bed, the food, the hospital gown. Most of all, he hated being away from Matthew, but Matthew was back in Marrell, staying with Caleb's parents, and he didn't particularly want them bringing him to Helena to see him because right now the way he looked... it would scare the boy. That's the last thing he wanted to do. Matthew had escaped his fall with only minor injuries, and he didn't want him subjected to anything more than what he'd already been through.

The irony of it—he hated that cave and everything it stood for. It was that cave where he'd been ruined. Yet it was also that cave that had saved Matthew after he'd fallen. Because it was warmer inside than it was outside. Matthew might have died of exposure all those hours out in the woods without his jacket. But all those hours in the cave had protected him.

"I hear you're not being the most cooperative patient today," Leanne said from the doorway.

She'd been in to see him every day, always hesitant, always very quiet, but it was truly the only thing he looked forward to. His body hurt, physical therapy hurt, everything hurt. His bad disposition didn't help matters either. "I don't like the food."

"Or the respiratory therapist, or the cleaning lady, or your bedsheets."

"They scratch."

She laughed, even though the look on her face showed clear discomfort. "And you're going to be in here at least another week, maybe two. So, how's that going to work?" She put a bag down on his bedside tray, then pulled out containers of soft food. Cottage cheese, applesauce, custard. Nothing that required much chewing as he couldn't chew yet.

"It's not. Which is why I'm going home."

She popped the lids off the food containers and handed him a spoon. "No, you're not. You need another procedure on your face, or you're going to end up with a crooked cheekbone. And

Sinclair Hospital doesn't have what you need to rehabilitate that shoulder…again. Besides, Jack Hanson's staying on for a while, maybe even permanently, to head up a real mountain rescue team. And I'm working there part-time, so we really don't need you back in any capacity yet. Not that you're in any shape to come back to work."

"Like I'm not in any shape to raise a spoon to my mouth," he said, fighting to tamp down his bad mood. He was angry—so angry with himself for literally climbing too close to the edge. But the closer he'd got, the more memories of that night had bombarded him, and he had been so caught up in those that he'd gotten sloppy. That's all there was to his fall. He'd got sloppy.

"Is that a hint? You want me to spoon-feed you?" Before he could answer, she spooned out a bit of custard and aimed it at his mouth. "Now, open up…"

"I can feed myself," he snapped, as he grabbed hold of her wrist to stop her, then realized he didn't have another hand available to take hold of the spoon, since his entire left arm was splinted against his body.

Leanne laughed. "Looks like you've got yourself a situation there."

"The only situation I've got is being here when I don't want to be." And memories. Ones he'd successfully pushed aside for so long. Had never put away like Leanne's had been. More like subdued. But now they had been unleashed, and that night was playing over and over in his mind. He couldn't stop it. Stripped naked, left there like that, with no way to get out for an entire night and most of the next day.

"I don't think so," she said seriously, shaking free of his grip.

"Why do I get the feeling you're about to do something I'm not going to like?"

"Because it's time. Because I remember." She sighed heavily and shut her eyes. "Because you're well enough now to listen to me, and I need to talk." Then she opened her eyes and looked directly into his.

"When did it come back to you, Leanne?" he asked seriously.

"When I thought you were going to die. Funny how that turned out. You said a trauma might have caused my condition, and it was a trauma that cleared it up. I remember what I did. I see it every time I shut my eyes now. I hated you so much..."

"But why?" he asked.

"Because we'd grown apart. Because you'd been the friend I'd counted on until Scott Mc-Briarty stepped in and took my place. Because you replaced me with him the way my dad had replaced me with you."

"I don't know what to say."

Leanne walked over to the window, glanced outside at the parking lot, then turned around and sat down on its ledge. "Maybe there's nothing to say. Still, what you did to me..."

"What I did?" He had no idea what she was talking about. He'd only ever loved her. Even after they'd grown apart. But by then he'd been smart enough to know that guys like him didn't end up with girls like her. So, trying to stay away from Leanne had been deliberate. But she had always been his flame, and he had always been her moth.

"Being friends with Scott."

"I wasn't allowed to have friends? Is that what you're telling me, Leanne, because I don't understand." But there was more. Something she wasn't telling him. Something that was hurting her. He could see it in her face. And, despite his frustration, all he wanted to do was hold her. Take care of her. Protect her. The same things he'd always wanted. Maybe even when he'd been married to Nancy.

"You laughed at me that night, Caleb. Up at Eagle Pointe. You and Scott. You were whispering back and forth about me, and I couldn't take it any longer."

"Take what, Leanne?"

"The fact that you continued to be his friend after he..." She stopped, shut her eyes, then rubbed her forehead. "After he attacked me."

"What?" Caleb nearly screamed.

"That night, when you asked me to meet you at Miller's Pond. I went, Caleb, because I missed you. I didn't care that you were geeky. I didn't care about anything except...you. But you were the one who walked away from our friendship. And, yes, it made me angry. So, I snubbed you, and made fun of you because I was hurt. It's the way a kid acts. All emotion, no real thought. But when you left that message in my school locker…all I wanted was to go out there like we used to do and skip rocks. I wanted us to be friends again."

"But you didn't come. Instead, you sent Scott to tell me you had other plans."

"I never asked you, Leanne. I swear…" His stomach was starting to churn as bad images began barraging him. And he was starting to sweat.

"But I had the note, and I thought you had. When Scott showed up, though…" She let out a heavy sigh. "He was pretty high. Acting crazy. Being rude. So, all I wanted to do was get away from him, get away from what I thought you'd done to me. Which was what I did. Scott suggested I stay out there with him for a little while, but I said no. He was a bad kid, Caleb. You weren't. Not until him." She shook her head and wrapped her arms around herself. "You hurt me. You shut me out. First my dad, then you. And there was no one else…"

"I shut you out because I knew the end of the story. Little-kid dreams turning into a reality that was nothing like they'd planned. I watched you, Leanne. You shone. People loved you. You had friends. Maybe not the kind you wanted but you were always surrounded by people who admired you, while I had a group of misfits just like me who nobody wanted around."

"But I did, Caleb. I always did. And that night, when I had so many hopes, Scott turned up..."

"What did he do to you?"

"He tried to rape me," she said without emotion. "Then after that, every time I saw you two together..."

His head was pounding now. Everything was finally making sense, yet nothing was making sense. "But he didn't..."

"Not rape, no. But he did molest me. Ripped off some of my clothes. Touched me." She grimaced, shut her eyes, shuddered. "Shoved me down, got on top of me..."

"Oh, God," Caleb moaned. Of all the things he'd imagined that might have caused her amnesia, this had never been one of them.

"What he didn't know, though, was that Jack Hanson had been working with me. I was strong. I fought back." She opened her eyes and looked straight at Caleb. "But I thought you knew what he'd done because of the way you two would look at me after that. Best friends talk, or brag. I was sure he had."

"Why didn't you tell someone?"

"Probably for the same reasons that over sixty percent of all sexual assaults on women go unreported. Some say it may be as high as ninety. I wasn't even a woman when it happened to me. I had no one to turn to. No one to talk to. So, it just went away. Got stowed in a place where I could go on without having to deal with it. That place you're calling childhood traumatic amnesia. At least, that's what I think happened. I'm going to need more professional help to sort it."

What could he say? What could he do? Other than to fight back the rising nausea, he didn't know. "So why me? Why did I become your target?"

"Probably because I thought you were betraying me by being friends with someone who'd attacked me. I mean, that's part of what I must sort out. But that night, up at Eagle Pointe, when you two were staring at me, laughing…" She moved closer to the bed but stayed at an arm's length. "I snapped, Caleb. That's all I could think. That you knew, and you were laughing about it."

"But I didn't, Leanne, or I'd have—"

"I know you didn't. I know that now. But I was a kid. I didn't know how to deal with what happened to me, and all I could see was that the one person I could have turned to had chosen to be friends with my attacker. Which was why I did what I did to you that night. I wanted you to feel exactly how I'd felt that night Scott attacked me, ripped off half my clothes and tried to…"

"Were you the one who sent help out to get me the next day?" he asked, wishing to God he could get out of bed, hold her, do something other than lie there and watch her suffer. But he couldn't. Not with the IVs and splints… And he felt like hell for being so helpless.

"I was. Because despite it all… I loved you."

She brushed away the tears streaming down her face. "Always have."

The words were barely out of her mouth. And all he could hear were the screams. *His screams.* Screaming for the things he didn't know. For the things he did.

And for Leanne. Mostly for Leanne.

Hours later—at least it seemed like hours later when, in fact, it had probably only been a little while—Leanne emerged from the hospital bathroom, cold water still splashed on her face, wondering what came next. Caleb hadn't spoken, not even when half the hospital staff had run into the room to see what was wrong with him. They were gone now, the door was shut, and it was just the two of them. Alone. Together. And she knew she didn't want to go on with this, but she also knew she couldn't stop. Not now. Not until everything was said. Because she remembered, every detail…every second of that horrible ordeal.

"I don't blame you for that, Caleb. At least, I don't anymore." He turned his head away from her but, not to be daunted, she sat down on the edge of the bed next to him. Reached over and took hold of his hand. "It's a mess. I'm a mess. You're a mess. And we've got a lot to work through. But the one thing I know, the one thing I'm sure of now, is that you couldn't have known what he did to me. Back then I thought you did. But you weren't like that. At least, not until I bullied you into doing things you wouldn't have normally done. Things to hurt you and humiliate you. Because I felt hurt and humiliated."

"That day, when they brought me out of the cave…" He still refused to look at her. "Half the town turned up to watch. They were making fun of me, Leanne. Saying terrible things. And all I wanted to do was go and hide somewhere."

"I know," she said, raising her hand to brush his cheek. "At least, now I know. Back then, though…" She swallowed hard. "And after you took it out on half the windows in town, and they arrested you…it didn't make me happy, Caleb. Didn't give me the satisfaction I wanted. In fact, that's why I left Marrell shortly after. Because I did remember that night. The look on your face.

Up until you fell off the cliff last week, that's the only thing I remembered. And I wanted to run away from it. Not from being molested. From what I'd done to you." With the back of her hand she swiped at the tears streaking down her cheeks, then continued. "I didn't know you would go off the deep end the way you did. If I'd been older, or smarter, I would have figured it out, but I wasn't, and…" She sniffed. "The trauma that brought about my amnesia wasn't about what Scott did to me, Caleb. It was about what I did to you."

All she could feel was despair, and loathing for the things she'd done. And an overwhelming sadness for the grief she knew Caleb must be going through now, and what she'd put him through back then. "I'm so sorry," she whispered. "I loved you, Caleb. Like I said before back then. Even now. It's never changed for me, even though I didn't remember it. But when I did…"

She waited for Caleb's response, but when it didn't come she finally stood, reconciled to what would come next. And she couldn't blame him.

She'd been a lonely girl who'd latched onto a lonely boy, and nothing had worked out. She was still lonely, lonelier than she'd ever been in her life. But Caleb had Matthew now, and she was glad for him. He deserved some happiness, and she was truly happy he'd found it. Caleb was a wonderful man. The love of her life, she was coming to realize. The one she'd never get over, and she wanted nothing but good things for him.

"I'm so sorry for what I did. Sorry that I didn't remember. Sorry for things I probably haven't even made sense of yet. I know you're not going to want to have anything to do with me now, and I don't blame you, because I don't want anything to do with myself either. But for what it's worth, you're the person I always knew you would be. A good man. A kind man. A man who didn't deserve to be hurt." He was also the person she had loved since she was five years old. And would always love.

She pushed the door open and started out into the hall, but stopped to take one final look back at him, only to find him looking at her.

"Would you report him now?" he asked simply.

"Does it matter, after all this time? They won't prosecute him. It's been too long."

"Yes, it matters. Because even if all you get to do is press charges, his crime will no longer be a secret, and maybe he'll lose some of that charmed life he lives. Or maybe someone else he might have done that to will fall within the legal time limit to prosecute and come forward. Most of all, though, it lets you move on. You didn't cause it, you didn't deserve it, and this finishes it."

"Except for more counseling." She sighed. "It *would* be nice knowing that *he* knows he didn't get away with it. Or that he won't get away with it in the future, if he's inclined to do it to someone else."

"Or just to get even," Caleb said, finally giving over to a smile. "You deserve your right in this, Leanne. And even if that right is only some self-satisfaction, it belongs to you, if you want it to."

"Why are you being so nice to me?" she asked. "I don't deserve it."

"What you don't deserve is what Scott did to you, and all the trauma that came afterward.

You're not to blame here. Neither am I. We were young, we didn't know…" He held out his hand to her. "We didn't have each other to help get us through it."

"You were always my knight in shining armor, because you were a dreamer, you know. Because you dreamed the dreams I wanted, and believed. Sure, they were little-kid dreams, but to a little kid they offered so much hope and promise when the rest of her world just wasn't working out. And, Caleb, I never saw you as odd or different. All I saw was…my friend. My one true friend."

"Until I wasn't."

"Until you weren't."

"I'm sorry for what Scott did to you. Sorry I couldn't defend you, because I would have."

She walked back over to him and took his hand. "I know you would."

"So, what about us?" he asked. "Can we work it out? Maybe come out on the other end with that dream we shared?"

"Would there ever be a possibility that you could trust us? Or trust me?" she asked honestly.

"When I first arrived, and knew you'd be here,

too, I didn't want anything to do with you. Didn't want someone like you being around my son. But you weren't...you. At least, not the one you turned into. You were more like the Leanne I knew when I was a child. But I didn't trust that. Couldn't. Because I was the one who *did* remember. Except I never factored myself into that equation. But I was there, Leanne. So, could I trust us? Or you? The answer is yes. I could, and I do. Although we're going to need help getting through it. If you want to get through it...with me."

"I do," she said. "For you, for me, for Matthew. I want *us*."

"But that means Marrell. Can you live with that?"

"Being in love changes everything. Didn't you say something to that effect once?"

"So, how, in any fairy tale ever told, does the ugliest, geekiest kid in town end up with the prettiest, most popular girl?"

"They say love is blind," she said.

He chuckled. "No way in hell it could be *that* blind."

"Well, for what it's worth, I never saw ugly or geeky back then, and I sure don't now." Not that looks mattered, because they didn't. Maybe that was looking through the eyes of love, maybe it was what he'd turned into. Or had always been. She didn't know, she didn't care. "Now tell me, what do we do next?"

"Could we start again, please? Go back to when we were five and six?"

"We could, but then we...*you* wouldn't have Matthew."

"I like it better when you say *we*."

"So do I. When you called and told me he was missing... I was so scared. For him, for you... All I could think about was how wonderful it felt having two people in my life I loved more than life itself, and how one of them was in danger. Those were agonizing hours, Caleb. I know they were for you, but they were for me, too." She swiped back her tears. "I knew when I went back to Seattle that I loved you, but coming back here, for Matthew...that's when I knew how much."

He sniffed, fighting back his own tears. "We *are* a mess, aren't we?"

"We are. But I think it's a mess we can straighten out, *if* you want to. But you must be the one to say you want to, because I've been standing here with my heart on my sleeve for quite a while now, and I haven't seen your heart yet. And I have to see it."

"You *are* my heart, Leanne. Always have been, even though I took some odd paths to get to where I could say that to you."

"Then we have our beginning, don't we?" she asked.

"We do," he said.

"We do," she repeated, sitting back down on the side of the bed with him. "But I also want you to bring Matthew home to live with us, let him commute to school even though Hans Schilling has bumped up security in huge ways. Matthew's part of that beginning, and I want us to be a family, together. I want to work part-time, help raise Matthew, take care of you...*especially take care of you.* If I'm lucky, give Matthew a brother or sister. Let you run the hospital, which was always my plan in the first place."

"Sounds like a good plan to me." He pointed

to the corner of his mouth. "Any plans for that particular spot?"

"Maybe," she said, bending in to give him a light kiss.

He scooted up in bed a little, taking care not to injure his shoulder. Then pointed to the other corner of his mouth. "More plans here?"

She obliged him with another light kiss.

"Maybe right there?" he pointed to a spot on his forehead, but when she kissed it, he sucked in a sharp breath and nearly recoiled from the pain. "OK, try there." He pointed to another spot on his face. Same pain reaction when she kissed him, though. Then he blew out a frustrated breath, reached out, pulled her face to his and kissed her hard, the way he wanted to. The way she deserved to be kissed. To hell with the pain.

"Didn't that hurt?" she asked, when he finally dropped back into his pillow, his expression caught somewhere between agony and ecstasy.

"Worth it," he managed to gasp. "Totally worth it. Now, would you call the nurse and ask her to bring me a pain pill?"

EPILOGUE

IT WAS HARD to believe. He'd been in Marrell only six months, and so much about his life had changed. Matthew had more friends than he could count and he was loving his young life in ways that excited Caleb. Ways that Caleb found amazing. But a lot of that was due to Leanne. She was loving life here, too. Working. Being a mother to Matthew. Being his wife.

And he was happy. His shoulder was healing nicely after a couple of surgeries. He was back to work part-time, glad to have admin duties to keep him busy when the physical act of being a doctor was more than he could handle.

"You know he isn't going to take no for an answer, don't you?" Leanne called from their cabin's front porch. "And he's in a hurry, Caleb. He wants to get up there before the sun goes down completely so he'll have time to get set for the perfect dusk shot. And he's right. The conditions are just right for it."

Caleb rose from the couch and wandered out to the front porch, where Matthew, with his camera equipment in a backpack, was standing, arms folded across his chest, looking impatient to get on with it. Leanne looked much the same. Meaning he couldn't win. Not where the two of them were concerned. They ganged up on him every chance they got, and dragged him out on one of their mother-son adventures. Not that he ever objected. Because he didn't. "And just what is it I'm supposed to do while you two are off taking pictures?" he asked, following them down off the porch.

"Look out for eagles, Dad," Matthew said. "I still haven't got a good shot."

"And carry the tripod," Leanne said, laughing as she thrust it at him.

"So that's all I am to you? Just someone to stand lookout, or tote and carry?"

"Poor Caleb," Leanne said, laughing as she stroked his cheek with her hand, then gave him a quick kiss.

"Now, that's the part I like," he said, grinning.

"And I hear the kissing's awfully good up at Eagle Pointe this time of year," she said, taking hold of Caleb's hand. "And other things." She pressed his hand to her belly. It was still flat, but wouldn't be for long. One night at Eagle Pointe…

Matthew turned back to his parents, and rolled his eyes. "Nothing's going to be good if we don't get started. And I promised Jenny she could go along, so…"

Caleb turned to Leanne. "Who's Jenny?"

She shook her head. "I don't know, but if he's anything like his father was at that age, we'll have plenty of time to find out."

* * * * *

LET'S TALK
Romance

For exclusive extracts, competitions and special offers, find us online:

f facebook.com/millsandboon

◎ @millsandboonuk

🐦 @millsandboon

Or get in touch on 0844 844 1351*

For all the latest titles coming soon, visit millsandboon.co.uk/nextmonth

*Calls cost 7p per minute plus your phone company's price per minute access charge